EXTENDED CLIP 2

Trai'Quan

Lock Down Publications and Ca$h Presents

Extended Clip 2
A Novel by *Trai'Quan*

Lock Down Publications
P.O. Box 944
Stockbridge, Ga 30281

Copyright 2021 by Trai'Quan
Extended Clip 2

Lock Down Publications
Like our page on Facebook: Lock Down
Publications @
www.facebook.com/lockdownpublications.ldp
Cover design and layout by: **Dynasty Cover Me**
Book interior design by: **Shawn Walker**
Editor: Shamika Smith

Stay Connected with Us!

Text **LOCKDOWN** to 22828 to stay up-to-date with new releases, sneak peaks, contests and more... Thank you!

Submission Guideline.

Submit the first three chapters of your completed manuscript to ldpsubmissions@gmail.com, subject line: Your book's title. The manuscript must be in a .doc file and sent as an attachment. Document should be in Times New Roman, double spaced and in size 12 font. Also, provide your synopsis and full contact information. If sending multiple submissions, they must each be in a separate email.

Have a story but no way to send it electronically? You can still submit to LDP/Ca$h Presents. Send in the first three chapters, written or typed, of your completed manuscript to:

LDP: Submissions Dept
P.O. Box 944
Stockbridge, Ga 30281

DO NOT send original manuscript. Must be a duplicate.

Provide your synopsis and a cover letter containing your full contact information.

Thanks for considering LDP and Ca$h Presents.

ARMOR PIERCING BULLETS

The most important thing to anyone is family. To Chalice, he's ready to die for his. Since meeting Joker, he's become a force to be reckoned with in the drug game. However, it seems like some people don't want to accept that as a necessary reality. As the Cartel launches an assault on Chalice and those close to him, he suddenly finds himself in a position where he has to acquire more power, but no one expects him to become *all-powerful*. When he meets Tereasa, a government agent who is a part of a department called 'The Ghost', Chalice is suddenly put in a position where he truly begins to understand what *real* power is.

Trai'Quan

Prologue

The wind coming in off the coast was cold. It would be considered colder than cold to someone who wasn't used to the type of weather and even colder yet for someone who underestimated the state of Florida and the Miami coastline. In the daytime, it would be unusually hot like the Sahara Desert in the summer. But at night, it was known to drop to the lowest of the lows. And only those who grew up close to the boy would be familiar with the atmospheric changes. Such was the case with the three individuals that stood over the body lying upon the dock.

All three of them somehow sharing a distinctive characteristic sameness aside from the three of them being dressed alike. They were wearing heavy clothing for the coldness. These three individuals somehow held a genetic likeness. The only real differences between the three were their physical structures and the fact that one of them was a woman. It was the woman that bent down and removed the tape from the bounded man's mouth.

"Please, you're making a mistake," the man gasped.

The woman smiled as she looked into his eyes seductively. Under any other conditions, he would have been turned on. Respectfully, this woman seemed to be more beautiful than life itself. Yet he knew that to lust over her was certain death.

"What makes you think that I make mistakes?" she asked.

"Do you think I'm stupid?"

The man swallowed the lump in his throat and felt the sweat upon his forehead, but couldn't wipe it away.

"I... I'm not saying you're stupid," he tried to explain. "But do you know who I work for?"

He watched as the woman smiled.

"If you mean the one that they call the Joker. Yeah, I know

him," she said.

"Well then you know what will happen to you..." he stated and watched as her smile grew broader.

"Let's just say that I'm looking forward to it," she said.

She stood back up and removed a gun from the back of her waistband. The man watched as she drew the silencer from her pocket and placed it on the end of the pistol. He knew that if the name didn't scare her, then begging wouldn't save his life. So, he took a deep breath and waited for the slug that was about to be delivered.

*****

Black Smoke found the body an hour later, washed back up under the docks of the marina. He took the time to examine the body for clues. He found the Tarot card stuffed into his mouth. It was the Jokers' card and there was a hole through the middle of the card. Black Smoke pulled out his phone and dialed a number.

"I found him," he said.

"And?"

Black Smoke paused before speaking. He looked down at the card he now held in his hand.

"I think it would be best if you and your family took a vacation. At least until I figure out what's going on," he said.

"You think it's that serious?"

Black Smoke once again looked down at the body of the Columbian and he sighed.

"Yeah... I think it's serious. Get your people together and head somewhere safe," he explained.

"Is there anywhere safe?"

Black Smoke thought about it. He knew what the Tarot Card really meant, and he had a pretty good idea who was behind it all. He also knew that they would have the advantage here in Florida, which meant that his people needed an equal playing ground. And honestly, no major city would do.

"You should visit your goddaughter," Black Smoke suggested.

"And put them in harm's way?"

He thought about the question. Six years ago, he'd gone to Augusta to help Erica's husband deal with the Haitian they called Big Afrika and his people. That small war had lasted nearly a year. But during that year, as he stood side by side with Chalice and his team, Black Smoke had come to realize something. What Chalice put together in that small city was very close to being equal to a real cartel. And in his city, these people wouldn't have the upper hand.

"The six of you should be leaving before sunrise. I'll try to end this down here. But if it follows you, I'm more than sure we'll have a better chance of facing it there." He ended the call and began to get rid of the body.

*****

Joker took a moment to think about the reality of the situation. The Giovani Cartel wasn't as powerful in the States as they once were and that was in part because his grandfather was getting too old. It seemed that the other families knew it too. There was war throughout South America, and the Giovani Cartel was having their own troubles there, so he couldn't look to them for help. And here in the States, the only family he had was very small. There were other people who might aid them, but no one he would trust. No one except Erica...

Joker dialed the numbers and spoke with his family. Yes, they could be ready before sunrise. No one asked too many questions. This life they lived... It didn't leave room for wasting time. However, they would be ready, and they would all leave as one. Time was of the greatest necessity.

Another Trai'Quan Original

Chapter One

It was hard to believe that seven years had gone by so fast. Chalice was having trouble believing that his life had changed so much. He looked to his right as he walked and watched as his son, Giovani, walked beside him looking all serious. He was an eight-year-old spitting image of his father. Giovani had the same thick waves in his hair and the same slanted eyes. The only thing different was that his skin color wasn't as dark as Chalice. Instead, Giovani was a mocha shade, a smooth mixture of his father's dark skin and his mother's brown skin. Unlike his six-year-old sister, Quintessa, she was the exact same shade as Erica and Pumpkin.

"Come on lil man... This is it," Chalice said.

As the two of them turned to step inside of Kay's Jewelers, Chalice stepped up to the counter just as the older white woman looked up and smiled.

"Mr. Scurry, we've been expecting you." She then looked down and said, "And how are you, Giovani?"

"I'm fine, thank you," Giovani responded.

"Has my order come?" Chalice asked.

"Yes, it came in late yesterday. One moment, please."

Both Chalice and Giovani moved about the jewelry store looking at various items. Not that they were lacking themselves, Chalice wore a twenty-thousand-dollar men's Dior watch that was the same as the one Giovani wore. They were both wearing Cuban link necklaces which were also iced out. Like father like son. Whenever Chalice thought to purchase himself something, he'd buy two, one for him and one for his son. They both looked up when the white woman returned and placed the two thin, long, velvet boxes side by side. Chalice watched as she opened both. Inside lay two pink diamond tennis bracelets, double brilliant-cut with twenty-two diamonds all set inside of white gold. One had the name Erica and the other said, Tessa.

"Thank you. They're beautiful. Could we get you to wrap them for us?" he asked.

"Sure, no problem. Just give me a second."

When she turned to go do that Chalice spoke, "So, you think wifey and your sister are going to like them?"

Tonight was his and Erica's anniversary. As he did with his son, whenever he bought her something, he bought something for his baby girl.

"Yeah... But what about Pumpkin?" Giovani asked.

"I've got something else for big sis. She's got a husband to buy her stuff like this," he said.

Pumpkin and Paris had been married two years now and had a son named Paris Jr. But right now, Chalice was thinking about his wife.

*****

Paris pulled his black Denali into the driveway right next to his wife's white Mercedes GLE. After parking, he and his six-year-old son exited the truck. Because of the so-called war they'd had with Big Afrika, Chalice made it an issue to secure a good real estate agent who helped them find six houses all in the same neighborhood. The only thing was, they were all in Evans, Georgia.

It was beautiful and not all houses were the same. Chalice and Erica had a four-bedroom, three-bathroom home that sat on half an acre while all of the others were only three bedrooms homes on smaller lots. B'Nice and Shae, along with John John and his girl, Alicia, lived on the same street. Everyone else lived further around the circle.

"Damn girl, what you cooking? It smells good up in here,"

Paris said as they entered the house.

His son didn't waste any time, he ran to his Xbox and ripped open the new games he'd just gotten.

"I'm surprised y'all home this early," Pumpkin said as she stepped out of the kitchen and into the living room.

Paris made sure to give her that 'I'm checking you out' look as she moved towards him. Pumpkin smiled. After having their son, she'd gotten thicker. With the hours she spent at the gym Paris owned, she'd turned her extra weight into a nice 34-25-39 and she had what was becoming a nice six-pack.

"I've gotta meet up wit' big bruh at nine o'clock. We've got some business at the clubs tonight, so I came in early to spend time with my baby," he said as he pulled her down into his lap.

"Careful nigga..." Pumpkin laughed. "I'm not trying to get pregnant again just yet."

"Shiiit... You might've married the wrong nigga then. Cause I know Junior can't wait to be a big brother." He laughed.

"Junior gon' be alright. He's got an eight-year-old uncle, and two six-year-old aunties, although one auntie was turning seven in a few months. Plus, Divine and John John's twins, so he won't be lonely," she outlined.

Pam and Cujo had a six-year-old daughter named Janiece, while Que and Kandy had a son named Divine who was five years old.

"Damn baby... You're taking all the fun out of it for me," he said.

"Don't worry, Papi... I'll make it up to you." She kissed him before she got up.

*****

"Sometimes I wonder why we let these niggaz live," B'Nice said to Que as they sat inside of his escalade ESV smoking a blunt.

They were parked in the parking lot of a gas station on the Hill. And while they'd been smoking, they watched as Cory pulled up to the gas pumps in his ole school '65 drop-top Impala with the music beating down the block like he was just that nigga.

"Two reasons, sun..." Que said between tokes. "One, we had our hands full wit' that Afrika nigga. That shit was more serious at the time. And second..." Que stop talking long enough to pass the blunt. "Number two, both him and that nigga Mustafa know what's up. As long as they stay in their place, fuck em. It's enough money out here for everybody to eat," he explained.

B'Nice heard his words, but he still didn't like it. This nigga Cory was now his problem. While Mustafa was Paris' problem. Neither one of them was acting up, but it just felt like their presence alone was too much.

It took them nearly a whole year to get rid of Big Afrika and his Haitians because every time they killed a handful, the nigga brought in two more hands full. And Big fuckin Afrika's bitch ass had been in hiding when he saw how they turned the heat up. Had it not been for Black Smoke, they might have still been at war.

Black Smoke found the nigga and clipped his punk ass after that they cleaned up the rest of his people. But the shit had taken too long.

*****

"Hello," Erica answered the phone.

She thought for sure it would be Pam calling her because she still had to go over there and pick up Tessa before it was too late. But when the voice spoke, all of her plans changed.

"I've got a problem, baby girl... I need your help." Joker's voice came across to her ear.

"What's the problem? Do we need to come to Miami tonight? I can get my mother-in-law to keep the kids," she said.

On the other end of the phone, she heard Joker laugh. "Slow down, baby girl... No, you don't have to go to Miami. Actually, we've just entered Augusta's city limits," he stated.

And Erica was vexed.

"What... You're here?" she asked.

"Yes, and the GPS says we're forty-five minutes away from you, so we'll be there in an hour. Right now, we're pulling into a gas station. Either way, I'll need to speak with Chalice and Paris," he explained.

"Sure, no problem. I'll call them both as soon as we hang up. Are you alright?" she asked.

"Yeah, we're alright. We'll speak about it once we get there and get everyone settled in. I hope we won't crowd you."

"Not at all. We have another house about half a mile away from this one, so you won't have to stay at a hotel. Whatever you need, we've got you," Erica said.

"Thanks, baby girl... That means a lot to me. I'll see you when we get there."

He ended the call and left Erica puzzled. She didn't know what was going on. But whatever it was that made Joker leave Miami with his family, it had to be serious. And if it was serious enough for him to turn to her for help, then that could only mean one thing. Cartel issues.

Erica called both Chalice and Paris and told them to come to the house as soon as possible. She told Paris to bring

Pumpkin and Paris Jr. with him. They asked if there was a problem and she said more than likely, but she couldn't say over the phone.

With both calls made, she wondered just how serious of an issue this would be. She was trying to figure out why Black Smoke hadn't taken care of it already. She prayed nothing bad had happened to him. She wouldn't have any details until they got there, so she waited.

Chapter Two

They were standing on the front porch as the two cars pulled into the driveway. One was an expensive Porsche 918 Spyder while the other car was a black Mercedes SL-Class convertible. From the Mercedes, Princess, her mother La'Donna, and her sister-in-law Drucilla exited followed by her nine-year-old daughter Carmelia. While from the Porsche emerged her husband Diamond and her father Joker.

Erica stepped off the porch and met La'Donna halfway. The two women embraced. While Pumpkin did the same with Princess. Chalice and Paris met Joker and Diamond in the yard. Joker took notice of both Chalice and Paris being armed. He smiled, seeing that they took no chance.

*****

Miami, Florida

The house was large, it was a mansion. There were a total of twelve bedrooms, six and a half baths, a large eat-in kitchen with a great room off to the side. It sat on six acres of land and was fenced in with only two ways in or out. Black Smoke sat inside of the car a good ways up the street from the mansion's entrance. His investigation brought him to the De'Grace's doorsteps because a few of the people he'd questioned mentioned seeing a woman that was too attractive to forget along with two other men and there was a very strong family resemblance between the three. The only local cartel family he could think of that powerful who wouldn't be fearful and fit that description were the De'Grace family. Their bloodline traced back to Veracruz, which was a city in Central Mexico and actually sat on the Gulf. It was East of Puebla and not a

19

very big city, but there were only two powerful families who traced their history back to it. The De'Grace family were the larger of the two. Their great Grandfather was called Pedro De'Grace. Having been a very small factor in one of the other cartels when he was a younger man, Pedro was patient and hard working. It was at the beginning of the Zettas campaign that he received his chance to really prove himself. Pedro would be the sole survivor of a convoy that was attacked along the trade routes. And because they were attacked by the Zetta's, who were once Mexican Military turned cartel, it was assumed that the Zetta's had killed everyone and taken the shipment of cocaine.

However, there were two things that weren't known. The name Pedro used while employed by this cartel family wasn't his own name. On the day of the attack, the convoy was hit by a very small force of Zetta's. During the attack, they'd somehow overlooked the small child-like survivor and made as if to recruit him into their ranks. Unbeknownst to them, was that this so-called child was a very dangerous grown man in a child's body. As the larger of the Zetta's force left only two men with the truck and set out to raid someone else's convoy somewhere else. Pedro, still having an old Smith & Wesson .44 shot and killed both men. He tossed their bodies out a mile further up the road. And that day the truck vanished from all existence. A few years later, Pedro De'Grace returned to Veracruz looking nothing like the youth that would have been remembered. Pedro now had a wife and a baby son along with so much American money that he was able to buy up a lot of land. This made him a very powerful man. Pedro hired ex-Zetta members into his organization and in turn, constructed his own cartel. His was built with more killers and thieves than thinking men. Pedro was the brain. Their first act of power was to destroy the family Pedro had once worked for and

Pedro took over their cocaine farms. Black Smoke knew all of this through word of mouth. He had no real facts to support anything. All of that had happened years ago down in Mexico. Here in the states, the De'Grace Cartel consisted of a very large family. However, it was run by three; the woman was the older granddaughter of Pedro's son. Her name was Justina De'Grace and she was known for being very brutal and ruthless. The two men were her first cousins, Fernando and Emanuel De'Grace. They were equally as bad as her, but it was Justina who sat at the head of the family table.

Black Smoke was trying to figure out why now did she decide to make a move against the Giovani family. Granted, Joker was considered the black sheep. Because of his half-breed status. But why now? He needed to find out what had changed to make this all a reality. Because some of the evidence wasn't making sense.

*****

"So, you don't know which family is targeting you?" Erica asked. She looked across to where Joker sat next to his wife, La'Donna. Diamond, their son-in-law, stood next to the couch they sat upon. He and his twin sister, Drucila, were both Dominican. Both were loyal to Joker. At the moment, Drucila was with Princess and Pumpkin.

"It's hard to say," Joker responded as he looked to where Erica sat in the expensive Lay-z-boy chair. Chalice stood at her right shoulder while their son-in-law, Paris, stood at her left. They were looking like they were her bodyguards, and she was the Queen instead of her husband and son-in-law.

"Black Smoke is looking into the situation. If he's able to, he'll solve the problem before it becomes a greater one," he

said.

"What about your people in South America?" Chalice asked. He watched as Joker sighed.

"I assumed Erica explained things to you. My mother fell in love with an American when she was sent here to attend college. The fact that he was a black man was considered taboo to her family, but they didn't find out until she'd made it known that she was pregnant with me."

At this point he paused, and Chalice excused himself. He returned with a bottle of Krug Clos champagne. He got enough glasses for everyone and poured. Joker didn't start speaking again until after he'd sipped his.

"Her father sent people to kill my father. They took my mother back to Santa Maria, not to her father, but to her grandfather. She'd always been his favorite grandchild." He paused. "I was born in Santa Maria. My mother returned to America six years later. The cocaine I get comes from my great grandfather's estate. For the time I was there, he took a liking to me. I've always been sponsored by his estate and not my grandfather's. My great grandfather passed away a year ago, but the business ties I have with his estates still stands."

This all made sense to Chalice seeing as he'd never seen many South Americans in Joker's presence whenever they were in Miami. Joker's circle consisted of mostly blacks who were from the US Virgin Islands.

"My grandfather runs the family now. However, he doesn't do direct business with me unless it benefits him. I do my business with my grandfather's brother, my uncle Diego. But he has no power other than that given by my great grandfather. Diego oversees the cocoa farms."

"Which means he doesn't have any American soldiers," Chalice summed up and Joker nodded.

For a moment, everyone was silently in thought trying to

figure out what would happen next.

"Well..." Chalice began. "You're good up here. You're family to us, so anybody come at you... They come at us. Now, we have the other house down the street and there's another three-bedroom house around the block where Pumpkin and Paris live. I'll have our real estate agent pull that one for Diamond and Princess tomorrow. Y'all can stay here as long as you like," he stated.

And Joker smiled.

"I appreciate that greatly... However, Just how safe is this area you live in?" he asked.

"Of the twenty-two homes in the neighborhood," Chalice began. "Seven of them already belong to us. I'll buy the eighth tomorrow. Out of the fourteen that are left, several doctors and lawyers live here. There's a bank owner and four police officers. One happens to be a friend, he's the Chief. Darnel Washington." He paused to consider his next words. "Only a fool would try to get at you in our neighborhood," he said.

"Yeah..." Paris laughed. "Between Chalice and Erica, they practically control the whole community."

"Trust me..." Erica added. "Your family is safe here."

Joker nodded his head. That was all he needed to know. Now he needed to talk to his Uncle Diego and make sure that things were still straight on that end. From what it looked like, he would be conducting his business from Evans, Georgia. So, he would have to restructure everything to fit the situation. He also needed to contact Black Smoke and find out what he knew.

*****

Chalice decided that once he secured the house for Princess and Diamond that he would call an official meeting with everyone present. He needed to make them all aware of the possible threat. He also needed to let them know who the new people in their community were because it wasn't a very large community. He needed to make Chief Washington aware of the newest members. That was a very important relationship to him. It had taken him a lot to build it. Chalice had ties with the Chief, the bank owner, Katherine Lewis, and her husband, as well as Judge Richard Sussman who also lived in the neighborhood. This is why his people were under strict orders to not sell any major drugs on their streets. If someone happened to have a small weed habit or snort a little coke here and there, cool. But no one was setting up shop, and no one was standing on corners. If anyone came into their community and tried to do so, they had orders to remove them. They were making too much money to lose by petty bullshit.

Chapter Three
Four Weeks Later

"I think we've found him."

Justina looked up from where she sat behind the desk inside of the study. Someone had just shown the private investigator she'd hired into the room.

"What do you mean by 'you think' you found him? Either you've found him, or you haven't," she said.

The guy swallowed the lump in his throat as he looked across the desk to the older woman. "I'm sorry... I mean, I know I've found him... It's just that the information you gave me didn't add up."

"...Oh. And how so?" she asked.

The investigator looked down at his notepad. "Well, you said the guy had no real powerful connections aside from a Diego Giovani who resides in Santa Maria," he read off.

"That's right..." Justine said. She noticed the strange look on the man's face. Something about what he had wasn't right.

"What is it?" she asked.

"Well... Where I found him, it seems like he has some very powerful friends. Or maybe they're family, I can't really tell." He consulted his notes. "He's in a place called Evans, Georgia, and the people he's with... Look, I've looked into them and what I found out isn't good."

Justina sat there looking calm, yet inside she was furious. "Tell me what you've found," she said.

She listened as the investigator told her about this guy named Chalice and his partner, who was also his son-in-law. What she heard wasn't what she wanted to hear.

"So, you're saying these guys have an organization that controls the whole city? What is it, Evans?" she asked.

"Actually," he corrected. "Evans is an outer county. The

city that these guys control is called Augusta. But it's not just there, it's nearly every surrounding county as well. From what I've seen, it is a lot. They have local law enforcement on their side. I'm afraid to tell you that going after him here, it's not to your advantage," he concluded.

Justina sat there fuming. She knew little of this Augusta. The place where the rich and wealthy went to play golf. They had no real ties to the city. A few of its people had come to Miami to purchase cocaine. But unlike Atlanta, the state's capital. Which she had ties to. She'd never thought they would need ties to such a small city. Other than old, rich, white guys, who wasted their time playing golf, she wouldn't have thought that Augusta had this type of people in it. Nevertheless, she made a mental note to look into the area now. Especially since her enemy was hiding there.

*****

Pumpkin, Shae, Princess, Drucila, and Alicia all entered another one of the clothing stores. Having been at the mall shopping for the past two hours.

"Ahem..." Pumpkin cleared her throat getting the other woman's attention. "Alicia, it looks like your little stalker friend is following you."

They all looked to where the guy who'd tried to talk to Alicia at the last store appeared outside of this one.

"God... Don't these guys have any kind of self-respect?" Alicia asked, sounding like the true white woman that she was. Alicia was John John's wife, and they had a set of twins together. They actually met at Erica's strip club where she'd been one of the dancers. For a white girl, she had the body of a black woman and even danced like one. However, she both talked and acted like a white girl.

"Well..." Shae laughed. "Don't worry about it, girl. We won't let the big, bad, black stalker attack you."

"Real funny," Alicia said.

They continued shopping and overlooked the guy.

*****

"Man, don't tell me you're following this white girl around?" Pig asked in disbelief. He looked back at the rest of his crew and said, "This nigga is love-struck."

He was talking about Big Mouse who somehow seemed to think that he knew the white girl from somewhere.

"Bruh, I'm telling you, the bitch used to be a stripper," Big Mouse was in the process of saying.

"She acts like she ain't know what you were talking about when you asked her." Zeus laughed. "Nigga asking a bitch bout being a stripper in the mall."

"The shit ain't that funny nigga," Big Mouse said seriously.

All three of them were over six feet tall, but Big Mouse was the largest. He stood every bit of 6'4" and weighed three hundred pounds even. They all hustled out on Travis Pine and 23rd.

"Nigga..." Pig laughed. "Quit acting all sensitive and shit. You the one got us walking behind these damn bitches."

Big Mouse didn't say anything after that. Instead, he walked along with them as they kept it moving. But he was still thinking about the blond hair white bitch he got the lap dance from a few years ago. He'd been looking for her, but it seemed like she'd disappeared or something. Yet today, he just up and bumps into the bitch only she was saying she wasn't the same bitch. The shit didn't make sense. He knew that he wasn't crazy.

*****

Pumpkin shook her head as she watched Alicia talk on her phone as she peeped out the window. The guy that seemed to be stalking her walked along slowly still trying to see if she would exit the store. Pumpkin kinda felt sorry for the guy because she knew what was about to happen next. And it was all because he said he'd seen Alicia dancing at the club her mother owned. He must've assumed that she had been into him or something. But even that didn't make sense because Alicia hadn't danced since she'd gotten pregnant and the twins were three years old now.

"Well..." she sighed. These niggaz were about to find out just how serious John John was about his white wife, the ex-stripper. That she did know.

"Who is she talking to while peeping around the corner?" Princess asked.

"Oh, you're about to find out when her husband gets here," Pumpkin said.

"You think he's going to show up because some guy likes his wife? Is he that possessive?" Princess asked.

"Oh, that isn't the half of it. John John is so in love with that girl, he might kill somebody about her one day. On the other hand, she's the same way about him," Pumpkin explained.

They watched as Alicia finished her call and put her phone back into her pocketbook.

*****

John John swung the black Navigator into the Augusta Malls' parking lot and hopped out. He left his gun on the seat, he wasn't about to go into the mall with a gun on him. There was no telling what might happen next. As he closed the door, he was conscious of B'Nice's black escalade pulling up next to his truck and both he and Que hopped out.

"Yo, you think we gon' beat somebody up?" B'Nice asked.

"Fuckin wit' this nigga, sun...ain't no telling." Que laughed.

They followed behind John John as he walked towards the mall. When he got the call, they'd been on the way to the park to play a few games of basketball. But then John John said something was going on with Alicia. B'Nice came along because Shae was pregnant. Que just felt like getting into some gangsta shit. It wasn't that often these days that somebody was stupid enough to try their team. Especially after all the exposure they got going at it with that nigga Big Afrika.

When they stepped inside the mall it wasn't long before they found the store where the girls were. But they didn't pull up on them. Instead, they sat down in front of the waterfalls while still making sure the girls knew they were there.

*****

When Pumpkin saw who came with him, she knew there was a strong possibility of there being a fight. If it had been Chalice or Paris, then it wouldn't be so bad. But B'Nice and Que, that was a bad combination altogether. When they left the store, she didn't speak, and no one acknowledged the guys. Instead, they kept walking until the stalker guy jumped out of thin air again.

"So, what's up girl? You gon' let me get yo' number or what?" Big Mouse asked. But he didn't say who he was talking to, so nobody spoke. They all kept walking.

"Damn Snow Bunny, you gon' just ignore a muthafucka?" Which was when Pumpkin stopped and turned.

"Listen... The woman doesn't wanna talk to you. So why don't y'all just go on and find somebody else to bother before there's some trouble," she said the whole time being very aware that John John, B'Nice, and Que were right behind them.

"Trouble? Girl, we like trouble. But shit, since she don't wanna kick it wit' my boy, what's up wit' you?" Zeus asked.

"I don't think her husband is going to go for that one," John John spoke from behind.

Pig, Zeus, and Big Mouse all turned to see who had gotten into their business. They found John John standing there alone. They didn't notice the other two guys who were looking into one of the store's windows.

"What?" Zeus looked John John up and down. "Nigga, who the fuck is you?"

"I'm the nigga married to the Snow Bunny," John John stated.

"And I'm just tryin to figure out why your boy been bothering my wife, but I can assure you that fuckin with any one of these women is trouble."

"Oh yeah?" Pig laughed. "And who gon' cause this trouble, you playboy?"

For a moment, there was silence as the three of them sized John John up. Meanwhile, John John looked at them crazy.

"Ahem," Pumpkin said. She looked over to where B'Nice and Que seemed to be arguing about something.

"Are y'all gone help him or what?" she asked, and the three men became aware of their presence.

"Hold up ma...." Que said.

"We trying to see who gets to fight the big nigga," B'Nice

said.

"But I think I should since I'm the tallest," Que said.

"Yeah, but I've got the nicest hand game," B'Nice said, and while they argued, everyone actually looked from one to the other as they spoke.

Pig looked at Big Mouse and asked, "Are these niggaz serious?"

"You know what...." Que stated. "Fuck it!" And he bombed on Big Mouse while B'Nice swung on Zeus, which left Pig and John John fighting. The women backed up and watched as it went down.

*****

The fight got them locked up and taken to the county jail, which meant that the girls had to bail them out. At the end of the day, they were charged with disturbing the peace, fighting, and causing damage to private property. But Pumpkin shook her head because all B'Nice and Que could talk about was how much fun they'd had. And when was the last time they had a good fight like that...

Trai'Quan

Chapter Four

In Miami, Joker had a large boat building business. By phone, he was able to shift people around into position so the business didn't suffer for lack of his presence. In turn, he decided to open his own restaurant in Augusta. the one he owned in Miami would run itself. He just had to use Chalice's Real Estate friend to find the right location. Through the woman who owned the bank, he opened an account and had his other Banks transfer money into it so that he could operate from where he was by wire transfers. He brought his wife a Mercedes SLS-AMG GT convertible coupe. While acquiring a Range Rover sport Evoque for himself. They had to be able to move around without it being a problem to anyone.

*****

Erica wasn't surprised at the way La'Donna fit in with her and Pam. The fact that she now owned two Clubs and Pam ran one while she ran the other. At the moment they were all seated in the VIP section of the newest club.

"So La'Donna, you go to many clubs in Miami?" Pam asked.

The three of them were sipping their drinks.

"I go to no clubs in Miami," La'Donna said in her best English.

She was originally Columbian and spoke more Spanish than she did English. "I'm surprised Joker allows me to go out with the two of you," she said.

"Gurl, please... You're too old not to hang out," Erica said while turning her drink up. "Besides, Joker knows I won't let anything happen to you. So, while you're here, girl have some fun."

La'Donna continued drinking her Serralles Don Q Cristal as she enjoyed the scenery with them. In more ways than one, she liked the atmosphere in Augusta. Unlike Miami, it wasn't too loud, and it wasn't as dangerous. Erica was refilling her glass when her phone vibrated. She pulled it out and wasn't surprised to see it was Chalice.

"Nigga, don't you know better than to interrupt my girl time? We're in the middle of having drinks. What you want?" she asked.

"Okay, Ma... my bad. I just wanted to let you know we'll be at Tabby's. And we might be late getting in. Let La'Donna know so she doesn't worry," he explained.

"Nigga, you called me to tell me that. You could have text it."

"Who is she talking to?" La'Donna asked Pam.

"Sounds like her husband," Pam said. She saw that La'Donna seem to be confused by the way they communicated.

"Uh, it's nothing... They both crazy," Pam told her.

Erica ended the call then sipped her drink before she spoke.

"By the way," she said. "All three of our husbands are at the poker house, so don't expect them to be home early."

There was a moment of silence.

"What does that mean?" La'Donna asked.

"It means they're getting drunk, playing cards, and losing money," Pam said, but La'Donna still hadn't grasped the concept.

"It means that we can hang out as late as we want to and drink as much as we want," Erica said.

"Oh." That, she seemed to comprehend.

*****

34

Joker had never played poker on this level. Tabby's was an old bar off Martin Luther King Jr. It had been around for a while just under different names. In the back of the bar, there was a fairly large room with two large round tables with five chairs around each. He sat at one of these tables along with Cujo. While Chalice sat at the other table. The stakes were pretty high. You had to have ten thousand to even get through the door. Luckily, they came prepared. Cujo had explained the rules to them. He'd said that this was where the old players hung out. The youngest person in the room was Chalice. But Chalice conducted himself like a man older than what his birth certificate said he was.

*****

"That's one nigga I'm about sick of," Mustafa stated.

And everyone seated at his table turned to look as Paris and another man walked into the waffle house.

"So, what you saying, Thug? We can light them niggaz up right now. All you gotta do is say the word."

Mustafa looked across the table to the young nigga who had spoken those words. Baby Nick was a tough young nigga. He had a reputation for slanging the iron. Then there was his man, Pocket Change, who was all about some paper. Rico sat next to him. Yet, even with the 4 of them, he knew the three weren't ready for the pressure that would come from fuckin with this nigga Paris.

"Nah Thug..." Mustafa said. "The timing ain't right, but this nigga gonna get his. Trust me."

Although he made the claim, Mustafa didn't know how he was gonna make his words a reality. He just knew that every time he saw Paris it hurt him to his heart that he had to share Barton Village with the nigga. He also remembered what they'd done to that nigga Big Afrika and his boys. Nowadays Big Afrika seemed like a name that was blown in the wind.

*****

"What's on your mind, bruh?" Diamond asked as they got a table near the back of the restaurant.

Having caught the way that Paris had looked at the large man with the full beard at the table up front.

"Everything's good," Paris said. "Just this nigga that hustles in the same area my crew traps out of."

Diamond glanced back up front once more. He was about to suggest they air the niggaz out. But just then the waitress came over and took their order.

"So... what I was saying was." Paris picked their conversation back. "If y'all gon' be staying in Augusta, then you might as well get in on what we've got going on."

"Yeah, I pushed weight down in Miami. But I'm seeing that you niggaz have a nice set up there," Diamond said.

"All we have to do is stay below GBI radar. Shit... Big bruh got his hands into a lot of shit, so the local cops don't bother us like that. But we don't do no hot boy shit either," Paris explained to him.

"I can find a nice spot. I'll set up shop then," Diamond said.

"Shit, we got a spot we've been meaning to move on. We just haven't gotten around to it yet. Spot called Travis Pine," Paris said.

Their food came and they continued talking as they ate. Paris explained how everything they had going on worked as one large unit. How they made money and lived good enough to enjoy it without worrying about losing it. And Diamond liked the sounds of that.

Trai'Quan

Chapter Five

When she arrived in Augusta, she got a suite at the Ritz Carlton and took a bath. Justina didn't normally travel alone but she needed her cousins to keep their eyes on things in Miami. Besides, she hadn't come here for conflict. She came so that she could see herself what they were up against. The suite was lavish, she had room service bring up a bottle of Chardonnay. Which arrived two minutes after she stepped out of the shower. Justina met the guy at the front door still wrapped in a towel with one wrapped around her head. She thanked him and handed him a fifty-dollar tip.

When she opened the bottle, she poured herself a glass and sat upon the nice Arabian sofa. Where she looked through the report the private investigator had given her. Inside of the report was a thorough outline of this Black Ayla/Black family. As she read it, Justina was at a loss for words. Having never heard tell of this guy Chalice. Although there were rumors of a guy named DeLow. How they'd been a black Bonnie and Clyde robbing team. Most of it she hadn't believed when her people brought it to her. But it was the guy Chalice who seemed to hold her attention. There was no real history about him beyond seven years ago. Or so the private Investigator had written. He nor his crew had histories beyond that. And to her trained experienced eye. That was strange. Especially for them to be at the level they were at within the game.

This guy Chalice had local politicians and Law Enforcement ties. From what she was reading. It said that he and his wife donated to charities and a lot of children's causes. They'd even open a youth development community center. Which was run by the wife and mother-in-law through the week. From what she was ready, if these truly were the people Joker was associated with then it would be nearly impossible to kill him without serious backlash.

*****

Black Smoke sat inside of the black on black Dodge Charger SRT contemplating. He'd followed Justina all the way from Miami and could have taken her out several times. Yet, common sense said that killing her wouldn't solve their problem. It was more than logical that she was receiving her orders from someone else. And if so, then they needed to know 'WHO'. He pulled his phone out and made a call.

"What's up bruh?" Chalice answered.

"I'm in your city. How's the Boss doing?" Black Smoke asked.

"He's enjoying himself. It seems like his mind is at ease. So, what's the situation?" Chalice asked.

"That's what I need you to meet me about. Can you meet me at the Ritz Carlton on Washington Road by yourself?"

"Yeah. No problem. Do I need to bring my work tools?" Chalice asked. Talking about his guns.

Black Smoke thought about it. Even though she'd come alone. He knew that she was still a threat.

"You shouldn't need anything heavy, but something just in case. Hit me as soon as you pull up."

Black Smoke ended the call then he waited.

*****

Chalice left the gym area of the Community Center and went to the office. He and Paris had been watching a few of the young cats boxing in the ring. Actually, one of his prize fighters was working with an up and coming sixteen-year-old female named Paula. So, when Black Smoke's call came through, he told Paris to take over. He tapped on the door then pushed it open to step inside. Erica was sitting behind the desk talking to La'Donna who sat on the couch. She looked up as he came in.

"I gotta make a run, but I don't know how long I'll be gone. It's some important business," he explained.

Erica twisted her face up. She looked from La'Donna to him.

"Nigga..." she began. "Since when do you need to tell me about every move you make? You just interrupted our very important girl time to tell me that," she stated.

He shook his head as La'Donna started laughing. Erica had her helping with the daycare and the teenage girls' outreach programs that she and Pam had created. Instead of speaking he backed out of the office and went outside to his Audi R55 coupe.

*****

"You always talk to him like that?" La'Donna asked.

"Yeah... It's normal," Erica told her, and then she noticed the strange look on La'Donna's face.

"Does it bother you?" she asked.

"No, it's just that in South America no wife would speak like that to her husband, especially if he was a Jefe. And certainly not in front of others," La'Donna explained.

"Girl..." Erica laughed. "That's just how Chalice and I connect. Him being a Boss and everyone else jumping when he speaks, he needs me to remind him not to get the big head and start making mistakes. Besides, you and Joker are family. I wouldn't talk like that to him in front of anyone outside of our family," Erica told her.

What she didn't explain was that she was the one who

made Chalice the 'Jefe' that he was. Technically anyway. Over the years he'd grown into the man that he now was. And that man needed to be reminded at times that he was still a human. During their war with Big Afrika, there had been a point where Chalice had gotten lost in his ego and she had to bring him back to reality before he made too large of a mistake. But she never brought that up to anyone.

*****

"So, what's the deal?" Chalice asked as he slid into the passenger seat of Black Smoke's ride. Having parked next to his and gotten out of his Audi.

"Joker's problem is inside. Seventh floor, room 712," Black Smoke told him.

"Okay then..." Chalice pulled the .44 Desert Eagle out of his underarm shoulder holster and checked the clip.

"A'ight... so let's go find the solution," he said.

But notice that Black Smoke wasn't making any moves. He knew that there was more to the situation.

"So, what haven't you told me?" he asked.

He sat back and listened as Black Smoke explained to him about the De'Grace Cartel and how his investigation led to them. But there were no real answers as to why a family that powerful would just up and target the black sheep of a less powerful family. There was no way that Joker could pose a threat to the De'Grace Cartel, especially when their power and resources stretched ten times farther than Joker's.

"Fuck it then... Why don't we just go ask her?" Chalice asked.

Black Smoke looked over to him.

"You make it sound easy," he said.

"Yeah... Look, just follow my lead. Come on." Chalice

opened the door and stepped out.

When the two gentlemen stepped into the restaurant of the hotel, Justina happened to glance up and see them. She already knew who the infamous Black Smoke was, and she easily recognized Chalice from the pictures the private investigator had taken. Justina continued eating her meal as the two men made a beeline to her table.

"Excuse me. Ms. De'Grace, do you mind if I have a word or two with you?" Chalice asked.

He stood there and watched as the elegant woman used a handkerchief to wipe her mouth. She took the time to allow her eyes to size both men up.

"Mr. Scurry, I've actually been looking forward to meeting you. Although I can't say the same for your associate."

She looked up into Black Smoke's dangerous eyes.

"He's been a thorn in a few of my business associates' sides over the years... But please, have a seat."

she waited until they were both seated across from her. Justina could also see the bulge under Chalice's arm, and she assumed that Black Smoke was armed as well.

"So, tell me... What is it that I can do for you gentlemen?" She finished with her meal and placed her fork upon the table next to her plate.

"You don't seem to be surprised to see us," Chalice stated.

"From what I've learned of your status here in this small city..." She smiled. "If I had to put the pieces together, I'd assume Black Smoke here has been watching my estates and followed me here from Miami. And since his employer is living amongst your people, he called you."

"Okay... So, you're smart. You've gotten my attention," Chalice said.

He glanced around at all of the people enjoying their

meals. "So, tell me... Why shouldn't I see you as an enemy and since I have the advantage here in my city? Why should I let you leave breathing?" he asked. Chalice watched as the attractive woman smiled as if she were the one in control and not him. That smile alone sort of spooked Chalice.

"Do you know why I'm here, Mr. Scurry?" she asked.

"Please... It's just Chalice. And no, I have no idea why you came this far by yourself."

Justina smiled as she looked into his eyes. Seeing the puzzlement within them.

"Neither one of you knows what's really going on, do you?" she probed.

And neither Chalice nor Black Smoke spoke.

"You see, Chalice... I have no issue with you. I wanted to see why Joker was able to come here and my people weren't able to touch him. Then I heard about you," she stated.

"I've never met, nor heard of a Black man as young as you are, having the power to back down a cartel."

Justina smiled. A true sign of respect in her eyes.

"Listen... All of that's well and fine, but you're telling me nothing. Joker is family. Which means whatever conflict you have with him, you have with me and I don't know how powerful you really are in Miami, lady..." Chalice paused to smile. "But here, in this small part of Georgia, I'd stand against the largest Cartel. And here, I have the home team advantage."

Justina took a moment to consider his words. Which she wasn't going to be quick to doubt.

"Alright... Here's the thing," she began. "Joker is no longer welcomed in Miami. All of his business ties, legal or illegal, from this point on is nonexistent. I won't try to touch him in your little city because I actually respect the way you have things structured. But tell Joker for me that he's old and consider this an honorable retirement."

"Wait a minute. So, you're telling me that you just don't want him in Miami?" Chalice asked, looking confused.

"Oh, it's much more complicated than that. I'm just telling you that the De'Grace family won't be a threat as long as he's nowhere near the State of Florida," Justina told him.

Chalice thought carefully about all of her words. Trying his best to see the bigger picture.

"So, what you're telling me without telling too much is that someone other than your family made the call. However, your family will only enforce it in Florida. Yet, there may be others who'd attempt to come here," Chalice said.

Justina smiled as she pushed her chair back to stand. "It seems you're actually an intelligent young man. I can see why you are where you're at today. Should you ever desire to make what you have here larger... Please, contact me."

Chapter Six

"It doesn't add up." Everyone looked over at Chalice. The meeting was taking place inside of the gym. It was after ten o'clock at night and standing or sitting around the boxing ring was Chalice, Black Smoke, Joker, Paris, Que, John John, B'Nice, and Diamond. At the moment Black Smoke had just explained to everybody what Justina De'Grace had told him and Chalice. Everyone had turned to look at Chalice as he spoke.

"I mean... She hadn't told us anything. All she did was hinted at the fact that someone else made the call on Joker," he said.

"Yeah... But we do know one thing," Paris put in as he looked around at everyone. "If her family is as powerful as Joker and Black Smoke says, then it would take some pretty powerful people to make them step up like they did."

"Maybe..." Joker stated, drawing everyone's eyes.

"Is there something we should know, Pops?" Diamond asked.

"I've been thinking since this whole thing started," Joker began.

"I've never done anything to the De'Grace Cartel. Nor have I directly bumped heads with anyone else. But it seems like someone had a problem with me being in Miami."

Joker stopped talking and fell deeper into his thoughts. Not paying attention to the fact that everyone was waiting. He sighed.

"About a year and a half ago there was a conflict with the Hernandez Cartel. Something had gone wrong between them and the Virgin Islands Tribunal, which includes all of the groups from the Islands who are involved with the criminal organized lifestyle in Florida. I'm not sure what exactly caused the conflict..." Joker paused long enough to glance around. "An assembly was called between the cartels. They weren't certain if the issue would lead to a war or not, but everyone's voice was called. I was called on behalf of the Giovani Cartel. My great grandfather used me as the North American representative," he stated.

"At this assembly, I disagreed with the move to go to war with the Island People. Especially with so little information to go, and..." Here he paused to look at Diamond.

"Not only is my son-in-law from the Islands, but the father that I never got to meet as well. He was originally from St. Thomas, which means I have blood ties to the Islands. I vetoed the move on behalf of the Giovani Cartel."

"If that is the case, it would explain why she didn't want to tell us who wanted you gone," Chalice summed up.

"But it doesn't tell us why now!" Paris threw in.

Joker thought about it some more. Now that he was using this line of logic, things were starting to make some sense.

"You need all of the standing cartels in an area to agree before starting a war on this level. If one of them votes against it, then it's avoided," Joker explained. "My veto was on behalf of the Giovani Cartel. A position and responsibility given to me by my great grandfather who passed away a year ago."

Silence followed after that, with everyone deep into their own thoughts about the situation.

"So maybe your grandfather replaced you when your great grandfather passed," Black Smoke said.

Having been with Joker for years. He already knew the circumstances involving his Great grandfather and his grandfather. The latter he knew cared less about Joker.

"But wouldn't you have been informed if there was a change like that being made?" Paris asked the question.

"Not really..." Joker told him. "If you lost your position it would usually be fatal. I'm guessing the De'Graces were supposed to kill me. But they didn't expect me to have a place to run."

Which made some real sense the more he thought about it. If that was the case, then someone would have to be sent to take his place at the table.

"There might be another problem," Joker spoke up.

"If my grandfather waited until his father died to disown me in the name of the family, then my great uncle Diego may have lost his position as well. Which would mean I can't secure the cocaine I've been selling you."

He hadn't spoken to Diego since right before the move was made against him. And he now knew that it was necessary that he reached out to his Great Uncle as soon as possible.

*****

"Where does that put us...?" Paris asked.

Everyone else was still out in the gym talking while he, Chalice, and Joker were now seated inside Erica's office.

"Shit... We've got enough Coke in the storage unit to make the rest of this year out," Chalice told him.

Having stockpiled enough cocaine over the years, had him feeling somewhat okay with the amount of time needed to score a new connect. But all of that would be gone in the next eight to nine months and the new year was in ten months, which meant they had at least six months to find another connect.

"Let me reach out to Diego...." joker said. "And if that doesn't work, I may have something else we could try."

"I can give you five months, but after that, I'll have to do something if we want to stay in business," Chalice stated.

There was no other way for him to look at it. Having built up an extensive clientele, there were people that depended on his team to come through with the product. Seventy percent of the people who brought serious weight locally got it from them. And it would be a major loss if they couldn't maintain their grip on the city. There wasn't any telling how many of their enemies were sitting in the cut waiting for the chance to take power.

*****

Mustafa was at the very top of that list. He got his cocaine from his up North Connection. And while he wasn't getting more than twenty-five kilos at a time. He was still straight. His connect could have doubled that easily. But Mustafa didn't see any reason to be sitting on fifty kilos or better. Not when this nigga Paris had access to a hundred kilos or better. Mustafa wasn't blind or stupid. He knew that these Black Family niggaz were also serving niggaz in South Carolina and maybe even North Carolina niggaz. There actually was no telling how much they really were doing. But Mustafa was waiting for his chance to knock these niggaz off their high horses.

But then again, he had some other shit about to go into play. Mustafa ended the call he'd been having and thought about what had been discussed. His cousin, Pig, had just found out that the niggaz who'd jumped his crew at the mall were this nigga that goes by Paris' team. And lil cuz wanted retribution. Mustafa had just explained that they needed to be smart about the shit because these niggaz didn't move like the average street niggaz, but he had a plan. All they had to do was give him a month or two. *Yeah,* Mustafa thought. *I'ma show these niggaz.*

Chapter Seven
Three Months Later
Duffle Bag Boys

BOOOOOOOM!

The door slammed open with so much force that the people inside of the apartment thought they were being raided by the GBI or ATF.

The girl whose apartment it was had been in the process of putting her kids to bed. While both T-Bone and Bo'Leg were in the kitchen using the counter to count all of the money that was lying around the kitchen.

"A'ight, nobody muthafuckin move!"

The three men wearing all white clear plastic face masks said as they stepped into the apartment with their guns waving. Bo'Leg had been in the process of removing a stack of bills from the counter, so his hands were filled at the time. But T-Bone made a break for the corner and pulled his gun at the same time, But he wasn't fast enough. One of the gunmen was holding a sawed-off double barrel. When he saw T-Bone make his move he made a hip-swiveling motion and squeezed both triggers all at once.

Boo... BOOOOM!

The sound in the closed apartment was so loud that it nearly made them all deaf. T-Bone's body pressed up against the wall, plastered. In the background the only thing that could be heard was a baby crying. Bo'Leg sat at the table with both hands up.

"A'ight nigga..." one of the gunmen spoke. "Don't sit there like you on the short bus. Nigga, bag that shit up."

"Man... Do y'all know who shit this is?" Bo'Leg asked because he honestly didn't think these niggaz knew who they were robbing.

"Yeah, nigga... And when that nigga Paris show up, tell him the Duffle Bag Boys said we appreciate it!" the one standing before him stated. "Now bag that shit up, nigga..."

The only thing that Bo'Leg could do was start pushing all of the money into the duffle bags the other two niggaz pulled off their shoulders. But inside, he was wondering just what Paris was gon' do about this shit.

*****

Paris had five money houses because he was bringing in so much money. B'Nice had three while both Que and John John had two apiece. Paris was standing in the living room of his Fleming Heights paper house when he got the next call.

"Yo, what up?" he answered.

"We been hit, big bruh... By some niggaz calling themselves the Duffle Bag Boys."

"Fuck!" Paris cursed. Because that was three of his paper spots that had been hit. "Anybody get hurt?" he asked.

"Yeah... They down bad T-Bone," Bo'Leg said.

"A'ight. Tighten up and tell Miesha I'ma make sure she good. Let me go look into this shit," Paris said.

He ended the call and thought about the situation. Of the five spots, three got hit. He'd collected from the other one as soon as the first call came through.

"A'ight Cam... Be on point. These fools hitting my spots think this shit sweet. But I'm about to see about that."

"I hear you, big bruh," Cam said.

Paris hefted the bags and took them out to his Denali. Once he had the bags of money in the back, he hopped inside and pulled off.

"I need to see if anybody else got hit," Paris mumbled to himself. "Fuckin Duffle Bag Boys, huh."

These hits started at a bad time. Joker had just come back from his meeting with Diego. Because his uncle wasn't 100% sure what his grandfather had going on, he hadn't allowed Joker to return to South America. Instead, Diego had flown into a private airstrip down in Texas. What he told Joker wasn't good though. Diego was no longer the production manager. His position had also been taken. His grandfather was advocating that he was restructuring the family, so a lot of people had been replaced.

Paris pulled his phone out and hit a number.

"Peace God. What's the B.I?" Que asked.

"Three of my bread stores got hit back to back by some clowns calling themselves the Duffle Bag Boys... You have any trouble, God?" he asked.

"Not that I know of... But yo, you need me to come through?" Que asked.

Paris thought about it. If he spazzed out, he didn't even know who these niggaz were and a lot of innocent people could get hurt if the Four Horsemen mounted up.

"Nah, just put the team on point. Let me see what I can find out. If I get some suspects, then it's good."

"A'ight sun, then get at me when it's high noon. Peace!"

Paris ended the call. Then drove on in thought. His mind was telling him that this shit had something to do with that nigga Mustafa. But there wasn't any proof. And since they'd originally spared him and Cory. He didn't want to go back on his word without some type of proof. What he really needed to do was get the street gospel. He dialed another number.

*****

Pumpkin listened closely as Paris explained to her what he needed. And she processed all of the information.

"A'ight. Let me hit the ladies and see what's up," she said.

"But yo.... make sure you take them all to Gangsta Twist and y'all be on point," he said.

Gangsta Twist was the hottest hair and nail salon in the city at the time. and it was expensive. But it was where all of the dope boys' girls got their hair and nails done and discussed the latest street gossip.

"And you're gonna pay for everything, right?" Pumpkin asked.

"Baby, didn't I just say that? You, Shae, Princess, Drucila, Kandy, and Alicia. I got y'all on the hair, nails, and all. But I need all of the street gospel y'all can get me," he said.

"Alright we got you, daddy. I'm a get on that now, so I'll get back wit' you."

Pumpkin ended the call and then began dialing up her crew. She already knew what they were looking for. And what the average dope boys didn't realize was, when they talked around their girls or bragged to them. If the girl was one of those shallow gold diggers. She wouldn't be able to wait to tell his business. Which was what they would be listening out for. because hair show gossip was now the new street gospel.

Chapter Eight

B-Nice walked into Walmart talking under his breath. He couldn't believe Shae made him drive all the way to the damn store for some pickles, ice cream, and a pack of Lance peanut butter cookies. He threw his chin up at the girl behind the register, her name was Nikki. She was one of Shae's friends. He bent the corner and walk down the aisle. He was in the process of getting what she wanted when someone interrupted his thoughts.

"That boy B'Nice... What's up playa?"

When he looked back, he saw Cory with his two partners Four-five and Rough Life.

"Oh, what it is C'?" he asked.

Trying to be cordial about the whole situation. A couple of weeks ago Cory had come to him asking if he could buy some weight. Because he hadn't been getting his work locally and DEA had the highways hot at the moment. Traveling was risky.

"It's tough, bruh," Cory stated. He looked to his two partners and said, "Let me holla at Thug one on one right quick."

He waited until they walked further up the aisle so that they weren't in ear range.

"You thought about that thing I asked you about?" he asked.

"I gave it some thought," B'Nice said. "What you tryna get?"

"I usually get two and a half when I'm on the road. And I was getting them at good prices," Cory told him.

B'Nice listened as he outlined it for him. When he quoted the prices he was paying, B'Nice was thinking that it was a few hundred higher than what they were selling their birds for.

But he knew that Cory didn't know their prices. Which meant that he could jerk the prices up and make a cap off this nigga. After all, they weren't pound up like that. But then B'Nice knew they weren't crabs like that.

"A'ight... Listen," B'Nice began. "You put six more G's with that, and I can bless you with three birds. But it won't be on no regular shit. I still got my other people I've been fuckin with."

"Shit, nigga... That's good business. One time or not," Cory said.

B'Nice got his number and told him he would call him with the details later. He excused himself and went to get what Shae sent him out to get.

*****

"So, we fuckin with that nigga's campaign now, Thug?" Four-Five asked as he watched B'Nice walk away.

"How many times I gotta tell y'all young niggaz that this shit is like a chess game? It's more complicated than checkers," Cory told them.

He'd taught them the game a year ago. Having learned it himself a few years back when he was in the county on a sells case. It was him learning the game that helped him get out of that charge. And allowed him to navigate his way through the streets the way he did.

"When you young niggas get yo weight up, you gon' see just how valuable learning the game is," Cory told them.

But he knew that these young niggaz out here in the streets now had limited vision. All they saw was the shit niggaz had. The nice whips, clothes, jewels, and bitches. All they understood was how their favorite rapper painted the fairytales of fame and glory that came with a mind full of finesse and a mean gunplay. But what these dumbass young niggaz didn't know was the truth about the game.

"Come on. Let's get this shit and get up outta here," Cory said.

As they walked, he pulled his phone out and sent a quick text.

"Gotta let wifey know everything is all good," he stated.

But neither one of them even thought to question the fact as to why he had to tell them he was texting his girl. None of that was their business nor concern.

*****

"Agent Williamson, I thought I told everyone that cell phones weren't allowed in my briefing room," the commanding officer said, and Gina's head snapped up alert.

"Sorry, sir. I forgot that it was even in my pocket," she said and waited while he paused for a moment. He went back into his lecture.

"Rumor has it that we may have some new players in the city. This guy, Chalice Scurry, was seen speaking with his woman a week and a half ago."

On the screen behind him, a woman's picture came up.

"Her name is Justina De'Grace. We've just found out that she is the figurehead of the De'Grace Cartel's North American distribution and marketing branch. Now, for years we've assumed that Mr. Scurry has been the largest cocaine supplier in the CSRA, but we've never had any real proof. This has left us wondering why how this upstanding tax paying citizen happened to be in the company of a cocaine Princess if he's not dealing in coke."

"Sir, maybe he's boinking her," one of the agents said.

"We've been watching this guy since his wedding six

years ago. He's only been *boinking* his wife. If he were a cheater, we would have long ago had proof of it," the commander said.

As the conversation continued, Gina lost focus. She was more concerned with the text her confidential informant had just sent to her phone. Apparently, he had something for her, and it was a good thing too. She was on the verge of pulling his ass in, especially since it had been a while since he gave her something solid.

Chapter Nine

Chalice moved like a man with a purpose. And his every movement was calculated in advance. He often prided himself on paying attention in class and was fortunate that he had himself a good teacher. Erica had sat him down after they'd killed Paint, her brother, and his boys. For a whole year, she explained and taught him how she'd been able to move undetected for so many years. It all boiled down to patience and meticulous thought, which was what he was going over inside of his head as he sat outside at one of the tables of the cafe and sipped on a cup of Columbian grain, straight black coffee.

At the moment, he was on the Cayman Islands, sitting across the street from one of its many illustrious banks. He was wearing a $3,500 suit by Michael Kors along with the expensive Marsell loafers. A $30,000 David Yurman watch with a $2,000.00 Phillip Stein cufflink. But he didn't come all this way to this Island for a fashion show. He stood up and greeted the two men that walked to his table. Chalice pushed his right hand out to shake.

"Mr. Giovani." He shook Diego's hand. Having already met the older man the day before to discuss the particulars.

"Mr. Scurry," Diego returned. Then he introduced the guy who'd accompanied him.

"I'd like you to meet Valentino Ramirez, Head of Operations for the Ramirez Cartel in North America."

"Nice to meet you, Jefe Ramirez. I'm Chalice Scurry." Chalice shook the other man's hand. "Please, have a seat." All three men took a seat at the small table. Chalice saw that Ramirez was a little younger than Joker. At a guess, he would say that this man was about Pam's age, about forty-six or so.

"Diego tells me that you have some production problems.

Especially since his brother has taken over their business."

"Yeah without him being able to help his great-nephew, it's placed me in a tight situation. Now, I have very few options," Chalice explained.

"And I'm told that Justina De'Grace might be one of these...uh, options," Ramirez asked.

Chalice was aware of the intense way that this man looked at him. And because he'd trained himself to always pay close attention to details, he was aware of the look. The same way that he was aware of the eight bodyguards who moved very stealth-like around the cafe.

"It's more like she's made me an offer. But for some reason, I don't think that I would enjoy being in service to her... uh. Due to business politics," Chalice stated.

Silence followed his proclamation and he waited patiently while it seemed the older man was in deep thought. Joker had asked that his great uncle meet with him. Having decided that it was about time that he stepped down and looked after his grandchildren. Diego understood the problem more than they thought. He'd explained to Chalice that Joker's grandfather wouldn't continue doing business with anyone who Joker had done business with. However, he'd agreed to give Chalice a formal introduction to Giovani and De'Graces' greatest business adversary. The Ramirez Cartel.

"Mr. Scurry..." Jefe Ramirez began, but Chalice stopped him.

"Please... Just Chalice," he said.

"Alright then... Chalice." Jefe Ramirez continued, "I've had some of my people look into your operation. And from what I've been told, it's a very lucrative operation for such a small area. However, it shows me that you have a good head for the business," he explained.

He allowed his words time to sit. He needed to be sure that

if he did business with this young man that they were both on the same page.

"But truthfully, Chalice, your operation is too small for my needs," he stated.

Chalice bobbed his head up and down, very businesslike.

"And your needs would be?" he asked.

"You were receiving what... A hundred to two-hundred kilos every two and a half months from Joker and Diego," Jefe Ramirez guessed.

"Closer to two. Yeah," he confirmed.

"I would need someone who could handle at least double that every other month," Jefe Ramirez said, and Chalice whistled.

"That's a lot of cocaine, and coming in pretty fast," he acknowledged.

"You see... In this business, every Cartel is fighting to outdo every other cartel," Jefe Ramirez explained. "What you may not understand in America is that our fields produce cocoa at rapid rates. Some of us have tons of cocaine in storage, waiting to be moved and distributed. But we don't seem to have the people with the balls and the power to move this much product. And that my friend is what I need. Someone with enough balls and the ability to handle the power that would come with the product," he explained.

Chalice was thinking. that was a lot of power and it would be a great responsibility. One that he wasn't sure that he could handle. As if reading his mind, Jefe Ramirez added.

"Here's an example of what level we would need you to be on if we decide to do business with you, Chalice. Right now, your operation, you're Black Ayla - the Black Family. You have the cooperation of the local law enforcement because of whatever moves you made to secure that protection, right?"

He watched as Chalice nodded his head.

"And if I told you that the FBI has you as a person of interest, that they're watching you and your Black Family as we speak. They are waiting for you to make a mistake and they're ready to take all of you down. What would you say?" he asked.

Chalice sat there silently thinking about this new information. A *person of interest?*

"You see... Here's the thing," Jefe Ramirez added. "There's a solution and it doesn't come by downsizing."

"Wait a minute... How does getting larger make me less of a target for the FBI?" Chalice asked vexingly.

"If you were to accept working with us, we would need you to become the major distributor in Georgia, both South and North Carolina, Virginia and Tennessee. With the possibility of expanding farther." Jefe Ramirez made a large circular motion with his hand on the table.

However, Chalice still didn't understand how this would work. It didn't make any sense. The target that would be placed on him and his people would be bigger than what they placed on Freeway Ricky Ross.

"Okay... Logic suggests to my rational thinking mind that you wouldn't have made this pitch without carefully considering all of the pros and cons," Chalice said. "So, I'll bite. Let's assume I've already agreed. How exactly does this work?"

He watched Jefe Ramirez smile. He reached into his coat and pulled out a cellphone. He placed it face up on the table between them.

"If you agree... I make one phone call and everything the FBI thinks they have on you vanishes right now."

Chalice looked down and thought, *That's a powerful ass iPhone.* He looked over at Diego, but the other man was just as quiet. This was a big decision. It could change all of their lives for the better. Then again, he wasn't sure if the family would be able to handle it. But one thing he did know, they were not prepared to handle a federal case.

"Alright..." He sighed. "But there's one condition." Jefe Ramirez picked his phone up and paused.

"Which is?" he asked.

"You obviously have some very powerful people in the States. Well, if you want me to successfully manage, control and expand with this much product, I'll have to meet with these powerful people to understand the security of my people. You do that and I'll be the biggest cocaine distributor America has ever heard of," Chalice said.

He watched as Jefe Ramirez held a finger up and then made the phone call.

"Yes... Mr. Chalice Scurry and his entire organization are now on our team... Toss the FBI thing." The older man ended the call and he smiled across the table to Chalice. He then held his hand up and as Chalice sat there and watched. People from the other tables began to stand. Men and women alike. They approached their table and introduced themselves... Two state senators, four superior court judges, several district attorneys, and no less than two FBI and CIA members from each of the states he'd outlined earlier.

Chalice met each one of them with a shocked expression upon his face. And he thought, *This just might work...*

Chapter Ten

"Baby, are you sure that's what Alicia heard?" Paris asked. He was standing there looking crazy at Pumpkin as she stood at the island bar. He'd sent them to the salon for three weeks straight. And this seemed like the only real breakthrough that they'd had.

"Yeah. She said this girl, Hope, was bragging to another girl about being a Duffle Bag Girl. She said something about her boyfriend, Zeus, was certified," she explained.

Zeus, Zeus... He tried to place the name, but he could think of nobody with that name. Nor had he heard it before. Paris turned and pulled out his phone.

"Ahem... Thank you, Pumpkin. You're welcome Paris," she said sarcastically.

"You know I've got you, baby," Paris said as he walked out of the room. "Diamond... Yo, you busy?" he asked.

"Not really... What's up?" Diamond responded.

"I just got a little intel on the niggaz who hit my bread stores. I'ma pull Que over too. But John John and B'Nice been on some other business lately," Paris explained.

"Alright, pull up and get me."

"Bet. Let me hit Que." Paris ended that call as he stepped into the bedroom, dialing Que's number.

"Peace God... What's the science?" Que answered.

"You busy?"

"Nah, is it a knowledge cipher?" Que asked.

"Yeah, them kids who ate dinner at my mom's place..."

"Yeah, yeah them kids who were being nosey and shit. All off in the backroom and shit. Playing..." Que said.

"Yeah... moms said to return the toys they left. But yo, I'ma come through in like fifteen."

"A'ight... Peace!"

*****

"Captain, I'm telling you this is a good lead," Agent Gina Williamson tried to explain to the captain of their field team.

But the Captain sat behind his desk, leaning back in his chair and looking up at the ceiling. He was paying so much attention to it that she almost thought something was up there. She glanced to the other two DEA agents who stood in the office waiting.

"Sir, we're wasting time. My snitch could call back any minute with the location of the meeting. This is our chance to get something solid on the Black Family," she pleaded.

"I heard you the first time, Agent Williamson. But right now, our orders are to wait. Someone is coming to speak with us. They should be here any minute," the captain said.

Gina sighed in frustration because she knew how hard it had been for their office to get something that they could use against this Black Family organization. And now that they had a possible in, Captain decided to drag his feet.

The speaker on the desk buzzed and the Captain pressed the button for it to speak.

"Yeah," he said.

"Sir... There's a Ms. Swoop here to see you. She says you already know what it's about," his secretary said.

"Show her in," he said.

And not a minute later, the door was opened and a nicely dressed white woman entered. The woman was no more than 5'5" and very petite. She wore an expensive Roberta Cavalli skirt suit, Giuseppe heels, and a Cartier watch on her arm. She wore no other jewelry, and she carried a Fendi briefcase.

the captain stood up to greet her as she approached his desk and put her hand out.

"Ms. Swoop... It's nice to meet you."

"Captain Thomas..." She shook his hand. Then she took the time to look around the office at the others. "This is your team, right?" she asked.

Captain Thomas nodded but didn't speak. Over the phone, he'd received instructions. So, he pretty much already knew why she was here.

"Alright... I'll make this real simple for you guys." Ms. Swoop began. "You've been investigating what is being called The Black Family... Well, I'm here to officially tell you that the books are closed on that investigation," she stated.

"What?" Gina Williamson looked astonished. "Wait a minute. What exactly does that mean?"

Ms. Swoop smiled at the older woman.

"It means... The Black Family, Chalice Scurry, and all others associated with him are no longer your concern. As of this moment, you're to stay away from them." She paused a moment to look around. "You're DEA, so you know that there are plenty of other dealers for you to go after. We've even found one that you should've been had a case on. This guy, Marcus Abelson, alias Mustafa... We found out about him pretty quick," she explained.

"I'm sorry... I don't mean to sound funny," Gina Williamson said. "I didn't catch it when you walked in. You work for which division now?"

They all watched as the woman smiled.

"Are you familiar with the title 'GHOST'?" she asked. "Well, consider the Black Family one of our projects. To confirm that means stay away from them," she said.

Gina sat there thinking about what was being said. Within the whole alphabet structure, there was only one faction that all of them were in the dark about and it was the Ghost. Rumor had it that the Ghost was made up of every organization. FBI,

DEA, CIA, ATF, NSA, you name it. No one could pinpoint which organization an agent was from unless they told you.

Of course, Ghost would never tell you. For all they knew, this woman could be a high-ranking CIA or FBI agent.

*****

Teresa swoop started the dark blue Nissan Nismo coupe and pulled out of the parking lot. The coupe was a $150,000.00 car and the engine under the hood was able to outrun any of the turbo charge federal vehicles. Her vehicle came with the FBI running lights and blinkers. Her position as a Ghost was one with quite a bit of power. having been the top field agent in her division at the CIA. The Ghost program was very much like the CIA. One of the main differences was, the CIA usually worked abroad. They had international spies. While 'Ghost' worked *everywhere,* and no one knew who they really reported to.

Tereasa had a lead foot. She often drove fast, which was the main reason for her owning this type of car. Ghost had their own budget. Their money came from the projects they invested in. And through this budget, they were able to dress the way they chose to dress, drive expensive cars, wear expensive jewelry and even live in expensive houses. Only a Ghost knew the details of what they were really doing.

She made a turn at the lights then got onto Walton Way. Her people told her that Chalice had purchased a nice three-bedroom house that she would be living in. her orders were to work out of the federal office here and to even assist them in their other investigations. But to make sure that nothing interfered with Chalice's operation. She would be meeting both Chalice and his wife when she reached Evans. She would also need to meet every direct member of his structure. With the Ramirez Cartel picking up the tab, she could live like royalty forever. Tereasa was only hoping that this guy Chalice was as smart as they said he was. That would make her job easier...

Trai'Quan

Chapter Eleven

"The fuck is going on...." Cory cursed as he left the sixth text. Still not understanding.

He whipped his Camaro Z28 Super Coupe through traffic. The money sat over in the passenger seat. He had it inside of a Nike book bag. Having just gotten the call from B'Nice about the drop, he was on the way now to pick it up. Cory was hoping that Agent Williamson received all of his texts. Having sent her the location of the drop, she'd told him that he could keep his money. She only wanted to catch this guy in possession of the cocaine.

B'Nice's people didn't sell crack. Instead, they sold large amounts of cocaine. To Cory's knowledge, none of them had trap houses, which was why it was so hard for the DEA to get any real good evidence on them. But one thing about it was, he didn't have any love for these niggaz. He was wondering why he had to drive all the way out to Thompson just to pick up the package.

He turned off onto the road that the GPS map showed him and followed down a few more streets. He eventually ended up at a house that looked like it was part of a farm. There were chickens out in the yard, and he could see what looked like a pig's pen. The house didn't look special in any type of way. But he definitely was impressed by the cars he saw. There was B'Nice's black Escalade ESV and a black Range Rover. He also saw the dark blue Nissan Nismo Coupe. Other than those, he saw the F350 sitting next to a Mitsubishi Endeavor. Cory pulled up and parked behind the Endeavor. He reached over, grabbed the bag and got out. The front door to the house opened and he saw B'Nice step out.

"What's good, thug?" Cory asked.

"What's up, thug?" B'Nice said as he stepped down off

71

the porch and walked over to meet him. B'Nice looked at the bag.

"That's your money right there?"

"Yeah..." Cory smiled. "Man, I'm sure glad we were able to set our differences aside and work together."

"Don't even worry about all of that bruh. Shiiit, yo money spends just like every other niggaz money," B'Nice told him as he looked into Cory's face. He noticed that Cory seemed to be avoiding looking him in the eyes. And he really hated when another man wouldn't look him in the eyes.

"Ayo... But before we get to this business... Come on, I wanna show you some shit out back." B'Nice turned and led the way.

"Man, what y'all do out here? Cook the dope or sell some shit?" Cory asked, following closely behind B'Nice.

"We've got several things we do out here, but you gon' like this shit."

At the back of the house, Cory saw what looked like another large pigpen. He saw Chalice and John John standing at the fence looking over into it. Both of them held a large hand full of money. He also saw a petite white woman with black hair and expensive clothing. She seemed to be into a deep conversation with Chalice's wife. Cory knew who Erica was because of all the old street talk. It had been said that she was the one that put Chalice on in the game. He also saw a large country looking black man with a cigarette hanging out of his mouth.

"Nah, I'm telling you the hog gon' win," John John was saying as Cory and B'Nice walked up.

"Why? Because the gator so small?" Chalice asked.

When Cory and B'Nice reached the fence, they looked in and saw that there was a massive size hog inside of the fence along with a baby alligator. The hog was at least ninety pounds maybe even a hundred, while the alligator was only five feet long and about half the weight of the hog. From the looks of it, they'd just placed one of them into the pen.

Cory noticed that the cute little white woman was giving him the eye, so he started smelling himself.

"What you think, Cory?" Chalice asked. "Which one you like for the money?"

Cory looked into the pen. This was actually the first time he'd ever spoken with Chalice because Chalice didn't hang in the streets. Cory looked into the pen; he saw the gator sitting in a corner watching the hog like a predator. While the hog ate his slop over in the other corner, he too seemed to be watching the gator.

He was just about to say that he didn't know when he felt the cold steel being placed to the back of his head. Cory froze and watched as everyone turned to face him.

"John John get his gun and pat his ass down," Chalice said.

As Cory stood still while John John did just that, he spoke. "Hey... Listen, fellas... I just came to purchase some product. That's all," Cory stated.

He watched as Chalice walked over to stand in front of him. Cory wasn't scared because he figured this nigga Chalice was too big-time to just make a deal without being sure the person wasn't on the bullshit.

"How many people did you tell that you were coming out here?" Chalice asked.

"I didn't tell anybody, thug. B' said not to bring anybody and not to tell anybody," Cory said.

He watched as Chalice looked him up and down. To him, it seemed like everything was alright. But he watched as the white woman moved to stand next to Chalice holding an iPhone. She seemed to be scrolling through something. Once she found what she was looking for, she showed it to Chalice.

"You didn't text this address to an Agent Williamson and tell her it was about to go down?" Chalice asked.

And it was at this point that Cory's heartbeat began to speed up. He was feeling a real panic attack coming on. Cory swallowed the lump in his throat.

"M... Man. Listen... It... It ain't what you think," Cory said.

Chalice stood there looking straight into his eyes. It seemed as if he was no longer speaking.

"So, you're not a confidential informant for Agent Gina Williamson? You didn't help her put away three other dealers, one of them being this guy Brickman who ran the Hill before you?" the white woman asked.

"Oh... And before you tell me a lie." He watched as she reached into her pocket and pulled out her wallet. She flipped it open and showed him a CIA badge. "Yeah... I'm a federal agent, so I know everything about you," she stated.

It was at that point, a certain sense of reality set in on him. Cory could remember when the bitch, Agent Williamson, said they weren't able to get any inside information on Chalice. And he now realized that it was because he'd been fucking with these people from the get-go.

"L-look." He swallowed hard. "Man, I'm sorry. They put pressure on me... I didn't really have a choice."

He tried to tell them, but it didn't look like anybody was buying it.

*****

Once they had Cory duck taped and naked, he tried to struggle as both B'Nice and John John lifted his body, tossing him over into the pen with the hog and the gator. Cory screamed and continued to scream louder as the Alligator attacked first.

They all watched as Cory tried to wiggle and move, but the gator wasn't letting up. The hog must have felt left out or something. Because while the gator attacked Cory's upper body, the hog set in on his bound feet.

"Which one you think gonna get full first?" John John asked.

"I don't know about gators," B'Nice said as he watched the scene. "But hogs don't get full. Them bitches only get bigger," he said.

"Listen..." Chalice broke the thought. "I'm about to take my two ladies out to eat, so I'll catch up wit' y'all later," he told B'Nice and John John.

"Oh..." Chalice added. "Y'all check-in wit' Paris and see if they need some help on that issue they got." He turned and threw up the deuces at the older black man who owned the farm.

Back out front, he saw Erica getting into Tereasa's car.

"Where y'all wanna eat?" he asked.

"I'm thinking of fish. What about you?" Erica asked as she looked across the roof of the Nismo.

"We'll meet you at Captain D's," Tereasa said.

As they got in the car and pulled off fast, he thought about the fact that Tereasa was bisexual. Erica told him when she asked if he had a problem with her exploring. He shook his head as he got into his truck. She also said that Tereasa liked him too, but he hadn't been there yet.

Chapter Twelve

"We may have a problem..."

Justina had just stepped out of her silver McLaren 650 Spider and walked over to where the twin Infiniti FX 50's were parked. Next to them sat an SLS-AMG GT coupe. Both of the Infiniti's belonged to her cousins Fernando and Emanuel De'Grace. The AMG belonged to the new Giovani representative whose name was Felipe Giovani. Felipe was Jefe Hector Giovani's youngest son. Hector himself was Jokers' Grandfather. And had gained control over the family once his father died over a year and a half ago. The first thing he'd done was removed Joker from his position and then Diego from his. Knowing that several of the families held some type of animosity against Joker, it was easy for him to use the other families to run Joker out of Miami. Although, the original plan was to have him marked for death. But then these De'Grace fools allowed him to escape. And since they couldn't kill him, the other families decided not to even try. At least while he was in Georgia. And Joker hadn't returned to Miami. That had all happened a little over six months ago.

"What's the problem?" Justina asked.

And it was Felipe who explained it to them. "It seems that this guy that Joker was dealing with, this Chalice guy and his Black family, have found another sponsor," he stated.

"I don't see how that is a problem," Justina said. "I mean, even I extended a hand to him. This guy seems to be a very impressive businessman. And I thought you people only wanted Joker out of the way," she said.

"That was the initial plan, yes... But." Felipe paused.

"The initial plan?" she said and looked into the face of her two cousins. "I don't like the sound of this."

"This guy, Chalice, has gone into business with Valentino

Ramirez," Felipe stated.

The implication itself outlined the possible conflict. Ramirez was liked by very few, but he was feared by all. All of the other families hated his ambition. Ramirez aimed to be thee Jefe over all of the cartels. The only thing preventing him from rising was the fact that the trade routes were controlled by several of the Cartels and everyone paid a tax to use it. Ramirez had attempted to take control of it several times. He'd gone to war with nearly every family at one point or another, but Ramirez was never able to gain a foothold. What made him such a threat was Ramirez owned a lot of land and not just any land. The land he owned was very productive, which meant that he had a lot of cocoa plants. No one family held more than him. If Ramirez were able to gain true passage into the United States, he could cripple the cocaine business for everyone. And he would have no compassion for any who opposed him. If they were ever forced to come to him for assistance, Ramirez would place great pressure on them all.

"So, Ramirez has no serious power," she stated.

"I'm sorry. I forgot to mention that he now has the full assistance of the Ghost," Felipe stated.

"What? That's impossible!" Justina nearly screamed. "What about our deal?"

"They've agreed to continue allowing our passages to flow as long as we continue to pay our taxes," Felipe said.

"But..." she asked.

"Our sources on the inside tell us that Ramirez had made a deal with the Ghost. He's paying a higher tax," Felipe said.

"How much higher?" she asked.

"Enough so that they're giving him free passage upon their own ships."

"Fuck!" Justina cursed.

With this type of deal, she knew that Valentino would be

able to move two to three times more cocaine into the United States than them. The Ghost had long ago come to them with this deal, but all of the families had refused. The deal would also give the Ghost more power over them. But with Ramirez making this deal himself, he could possibly put them all out of business. He would no longer need control of their trade routes to do it.

"We need to get rid of this guy Chalice... And soon," Felipe stated.

"That may not be as easy as it sounds. Especially if he's now under the protection of the Ghost." She informed him.

"We don't have a choice... The Assembly will be meeting within the next seventy-two hours. They will decide then how great of a threat this guy is. And what steps are to be taken."

Justina thought about that. Having looked into this guy herself, she didn't think that this would be as easy as the Assembly would think.

Trai'Quan

Chapter Thirteen

Never before in his life had he ever experienced anything like it. If there really was a heaven, Chalice thought that he'd just found it. He lay on his side, propped up on an elbow, smoking a blunt as he watched the two women roll around the bed naked. Most niggaz he knew only dreamed about this type of shit. He'd already fucked both of them. At first, he asked Erica just to be sure if this was the same thing as cheating. But she'd said that in this game, at the level he was at now, he would have thoughts about entertaining other women. She knew that. But she said that she wouldn't be able to accept him fucking around with any bitch that wasn't as boss as she was. Erica said that she considered Tereasa to be a 'Boss Bitch', and now she was their boss bitch.

"Look at him over there," Erica said into Tereasa's ear as she sucked on her neck and earlobes as if she were a vampire. "Looking all sexy, smoking his blunt."

He watched as her right hand slid down and she began to play with Tereasa's clit. Erica held eye contact with him as she stroked the bud and Tereasa moaned, enjoying the sensation.

"You know this pussy belongs to me and him now, don't you?" she asked.

"Yes," Tereasa spoke slightly above a whisper.

"That means..." Erica turned Tereasa's head so that she could look into the other woman's eyes. "If you ever want to get your back blown out, it's that dick that'll do it. And his alone. No other dicks go up in here." She pushed her fingers up into Tereasa. "You got a problem with that?" she asked.

Tereasa shook her head and moaned at the same time.

"Ugh, unn-unn... I can't hear you," Erica said. "Do you have a problem with this being our pussy exclusively? Chalice has the only dick that goes inside... And I'm the only woman that gets to play in it. So, I repeat. Do you have a problem with that?"

Tereasa opened her eyes and looked straight into Erica's.

"No," she said as she licked her lips. "I don't have a problem with that."

Her hips lifted as Erica found her spot and began to dig in deep.

"Good. Because I don't share with anybody but him. And he doesn't share with any other dicks. Now come on, let mama suck on that pearl."

Having made her point, Chalice watched as she adjusted her body so that she was between Tereasa's thighs. His eye's caught sight of the twin ladies' Rolexes that they both wore. Tereasa said that she hadn't been in the habit of wearing jewelry, but she would wear whatever Chalice brought her. He'd given her two pieces, the watch which matched the one he gave Erica and the red gold wedding band with the fifteen diamonds inside of it. The only difference between her ring and Erica's was that Erica's ring held sixteen diamonds, which signified her seniority.

Erica explained to him that a woman with Tereasa's power was a woman they needed to lock in completely. She said there was no telling if they would ever fall out with Ramirez in the future. But with Teresa permanently on their team. It wouldn't matter. Erica was making plans for the future.

*****

"Sun... If we know these niggaz in the ones, then why we ain't dead these niggaz yet?" Que said.

He was sitting in the passenger seat smoking a Newport. Diamond was quietly sitting in the back, but they were waiting on Paris to speak. After all, this was his business.

They were watching the trap house on Travis Pine. This was where the Duffle Bag Boys made their money when they weren't out robbing. They were some dope boys too. The only problem was these were Mustafa's cousins.

"You remember what Tereasa said," Paris reminded.

"Oh yeah... shit," Que said.

Because at the moment Mustafa was inside of the house. When Tereasa made her presence known to the entire Black Family one of the things she told them was that she was there to make sure they didn't have any problems with Law Enforcement of any level. From the FBI, DEA, ATF, or local police. But she'd said for her to be effective in doing this, they couldn't work against the things she set into motion. Tereasa had asked if they had any dealings with Mustafa. She said that he was currently the person of interest that she was giving the FBI. Because they were mad that they couldn't have the Black Family. So as a gift. She was helping them get Mustafa and his connection. Which meant that they couldn't touch Mustafa himself.

"We gon' pull up when this nigga ain't around," Paris told them as he started the SUV. "Don't worry, them niggaz gone feel it," he added.

*****

"So, listen cuz," Mustafa said as he stood in one of the back rooms talking to Pig. "I'ma need you niggaz to lay low. My plug is about to hit me with these seventy-five bricks, and I need to move 'em as fast as I can," he said to the younger man.

This was his third time getting seventy-five bricks from Franko Marcino. The only thing he didn't like about the whole plug situation was that he had to drive down to Tampa, Florida to pick up the bricks. And he hated to be on the road with that much work. The only good thing about it was his baby's mama, Latoria, would be riding with him. Her being an officer at Phinizy Road, she would be able to flash her badge. If ever they got pulled over, she would drop that on the cops, and they would let her go. The shit had happened twice back when he'd first started and was only getting ten bricks at a time. But his shit changed over two years ago when he met Franko. Now, he was almost at the hundred-kilo mark.

"I'ma pull you niggaz over when I get back, so y'all just keep your noses clean," Mustafa said. "And fall back on that Paris nigga. I think he has learned his lesson." They both laughed.

Mustafa gave his little cousin a pound and turned to leave the room. He actually had some other shit to do before they left to head south. Latoria was crying that she wanted a few new outfits before they left, and he had to keep the bitch happy. She was his safety ticket. Without her, his chances got very low.

Chapter Fourteen

"I don't get it," Agent Gina Williamson said. "We've never received any intel saying this guy was that large of a player. He can't be moving any more than ten kilos."

She looked to where Agent Swoop stood in the front of the room. Looking all super sexy in her Valente suit with Gucci heels. On her arm, she wore a Rolex. Gina also noticed her wedding ring this time. She hadn't seen one on her hand before.

Tereasa was beginning to see that this bitch was a problem, but she brushed it off. She had something for her though.

"Did your CI's inform you that this guy Mustafa was buying his cocaine from Franco Marcina?" she asked.

Tereasa saw the look that came to her face.

"Franko Marcina is the real target, guys." She looked around the room at the ten FBI and DEA agents present. "This guy, Mustafa, is just a plus. Franko is the stateside representative for the Marcina Cartel. If we can put Franko away, it would be bigger than anything you guys have done thus far. We get Franko... You guys get a promotion." she said.

"Ma'am... uh. What type of promotion?" One of the guys asked.

"Well, we're currently in the process of building an Eastern Task Force division. Our targets will be these stateside representatives of the South American Cartel," Tereasa explained to the entire room. "This task force will be limited in how many people are chosen to be on it. How you guys function on this takedown will determine if you receive a position on this team."

She made sure to stare hard at Agent Williamson, whom

she knew wouldn't be on the team. In fact, she was having her relocated altogether. *Agent Williamson didn't know how to keep her fuckin mouth shut,* Tereasa thought.

*****

Chalice looked over the list of profiles that Tereasa had gotten him. Seeing as feeding snitches wasn't the only thing that they used Big Lou's farm for. In the basement of Big Lou's house, Chalice had brought in a small crew of contractors who he had built another level downward. Nine feet further down there was a room, not a very large room, but big enough to be a walk-in closet. Within this room was where Chalice kept the six hundred kilos of cocaine that Ramirez had his people deliver to him. And that was a lot of coke.

This is why he'd asked Tereasa to use her resources to find him four major players. One in each of the four states that he was about to visit. The profiles had various information on each guy. And it was so thorough that Chalice wondered why dope boys thought they were below the radar.

There was a guy in Columbia, South Carolina named Big June. A large guy with a football player build. He was currently receiving fifteen kilos that he had to drive to Florida to get himself.

In Charlotte, North Carolina, there was a guy named Prince. He was touching close to twenty kilos. In Memphis, Tennessee there was a Gangster Disciple named King G. He was doing just over twenty. And in Virginia, an Asian guy named Tran was only getting ten kilos.

He would actually have to go spend some time in each one of these states. He needed to get to know each one of these guys and he needed them to know him. He just needed to figure out who he was gone take with him. Paris might have that bullshit wrapped up by then. But then again Paris was second in command and somebody needed to be available in case something happened. Both Que and Diamond were working with Paris, so he could count them out which only left B'Nice, John John, and Black Smoke.

Since Joker opened his restaurant, there didn't seem to be much for Black Smoke to do. He said he wasn't returning to Miami. Things down there didn't look so good he said, so he hung around. That was a good four-man team.

*****

"How much is it, thug?" Pig asked.

He stood and made his way to the kitchen where he opened the freezer, reached inside, and got another beer. They had just robbed some nigga up in Apple Valley who was slippin'. Their whole Duffle Bag Boys reign was being heard throughout the streets. And the funny part about it was they really didn't have to rob. Mustafa gave them enough food to keep their weight up. Robbing was something they just got off on doing.

"Man, that nigga only had $63,000," Zeus said after he finished counting the money. "I thought you said the nigga would have over two-hundred bands," he said.

"That's what that lil bitch, Taniesha, told me. You know she be fuckin' that nigga."

"What y'all niggaz trippin' bout?" Big Mouse came out of the bathroom. They could still hear the toilet flushing.

"It ain't but sixty bands, not two-hundred," Zeus said.

"So..." Big Mouse said. "It's all free money to me. Where that loud pack at?"

The money sat out in neat stacks on the coffee table. Zeus leaned forward and reached out for the bag of weed.

BOOM!

The door was kicked in with so much force that all of them stood there frozen at first. When the canister came through it, they didn't know what was going on.

BANG!

There was a loud explosion and a bright flash of light. The light blinded them, and the explosion left their ears ringing. Big Mouse fell to the floor clutching his head. Pig dropped his beer and fell back into the wall. And Zeus curled up on the sofa.

None of them even noticed when the three figures entered the apartment. All three of them wearing ski masks and holding guns. As they moved into the apartment, they let off shots. Killing the whole Duffle Bag Boys crew dead.

"What about the loot?" Que asked.

"Bag that shit back up. We ain't got but a couple of minutes," Paris said.

They used the same duffle bags as they gathered up all of the money lying around, and they headed back out just as quickly as they came. The whole hit took less than four minutes. By the time people in the other apartments realized what was going on, the small hit team had been in and out then were gone.

"And that..." Paris mumbled as they reached the SUV. "...is how you pull a jack move."

Chapter Fifteen

Another reason why he was able to successfully drive all the way back with a lot of dope in the car was because he didn't ride the highway back. Mustafa thought about that as he drove to Tampa. Latoria was asleep over in the passenger seat. He knew she was tired; she should be. The bitch had him running all over the mall spending his money. There wasn't anything that he could do about it because he really needed the bitch bad this time. He kinda blamed himself because he'd stressed how important this drive was to her. She even laid her uniform across the back seat. So, if they were pulled over, the cop would see it as soon as he walked up to the car. He had to admit the bitch knew what she was doing.

He crossed over into Florida when his phone buzzed. He pulled it out and read the text.

"Muthafucka..." he cursed.

"Wh-what?" Latoria shook out of her sleep.

"Oh nah... My bad boo," he said.

"The fuck you mad about now?" she asked.

"This nigga Red just texted me. Some muthafuckaz done ran up in Shani's apartment and killed Pig, Zeus, and Big Mouse."

"What? All three of em? What about Shani and the kids?" she asked.

"Shani wasn't home, so her and the kids should be straight."

I told them niggaz to lay low, he said inside of his mind. However, he knew they had blown up the spot with this Duffle Bag Boys shit. The sad thing was that they didn't even have to do that shit. He was gon' bless each one of them if they had waited.

*****

Gina Williamson was still in her feelings because she felt like she'd put too much work into going after the Black Family. And out of the blue, they were told that they couldn't push the case. On top of all that, her snitch had gone missing.

She looked out of the windshield to where the Nismo led the way. They'd just arrived in Tampa, Florida, and were about to meet up with the rest of Ms. Swoop's team. Gina knew that something had happened to Cory, but she couldn't prove it. And if she didn't know any better, she'd swear that this bitch had something to do with it.

The two Tahoes following the Nismo pulled into the parking lot of the Sun Inn. They all drove to the back of the lot where they saw the Frito Lays truck and the three Navigators. They all parked and stepped out. Gina followed her teammates as they all met at the back of the Frito's truck. The back door opened and a tall older white guy with grey hair stood there.

"Alright people, my name is Beck. No last name needed because after this operation some of you won't need to know it anyway." Beck looked around at all of the agents standing out in the parking lot.

"Alright here's the situation," Beck began. "This is Agent Swoop's baby, so today you all work for her. She only reports to me, no one else. If she gives you an order, don't question it. Just assume I gave the order. If you have a problem following instructions, then you can go back home, Now, any questions?" he asked then glanced around. No one spoke.

"Alright then... Agent Swoop." He turned it over to her.

"We're here to apprehend, capture, and arrest one of the North American Cartel representatives. Now, they'll be in the midst of a large drug deal which we'll seize as well," she outlined.

She went on to explain the details of what to expect during the seizure. When she finished, she put together three teams and told each one what she expected them to do. And for some reason, Gina found herself on the same team as Agent Swoop.

*****

The deal was going down in the Tampa Bay Marina. And it was long after 10:00 pm. All of the dock operators were gone home. The only one who was still around were those who made their boats their homes.

Mustafa carried the suitcase as he approached the docks. He knew exactly what he was looking for, having been here a few times before. As he continued his journey, he saw it approaching. The boat was a large silver Catamaran. One of those that had two staterooms fully loaded with queen-sized beds. He saw the lights were on as he reached the boat. Mustafa wasn't surprised to see the average size middle-aged man step out onto the deck. He stopped and looked up as the older man, smiled, and then it seemed like the four bodyguards materialized out of thin air.

Mustafa stood still while they searched him. He already knew the routine, so he held his tongue until they were finished.

Mustafa stepped onto the plank and walked up to board the boat.

"You got somewhere I can put this down? It's kinda heavy," Mustafa said about the suitcase.

"Just bring it downstairs. Come on." Franko led the way, and they went down into the hatch. When he got downstairs, he saw several women in bikinis walking around with drinks in their hands. Franko stopped one and asked her to take the suitcase. He moved over to the bar and fixed two drinks. Mustafa was really feeling himself. He was well on his way to balling big. It was only a matter of time.

*****

"Team one, move in," Agent Swoop said. "Remember, I need the two targets alive."

She glanced back to her team. There shouldn't be any need for them to do too much. Team One was actually made up of ex-Navy seals and Army Rangers. They too were Ghost, and just like everyone else, had been chosen because they were the best at what they did. In the distance, Tereasa heard the brief gunfire exchange. Two minutes later, the voice called into her ear.

"All clear mother..."

"Alright... Come on, guys." She turned and led her team to the match.

When they stepped on deck, all of her agents had their guns out. But she didn't. Tereasa looked to the team leader who stood over the two men bound and lying face-first on deck.

"What all did we get?" she asked.

"A lot," the team leader said.

She watched as the rest of the team brought out first the suitcase with all of the money. They brought out several bags with the cocaine individually wrapped inside of them one by one.

"Now that's what I call big business," Tereasa said over her shoulder towards those who were with her.

She took the time to look over the money and the cocaine good before she moved over to Franko.

"Franko Marcina. You have anything you wanna say

before we book your ass?" she asked.

"Fuck you, bitch. You and all of your spook friends," he stated.

"Aww... you wanna talk all sweet and shit," Tereasa said. "But guess what Franko? You won't be lonely where you're going because I'm going to put your whole fuckin Assembly in there with you," she told him. "I thought you guys were smart. You should have played ball when you had the chance to. Now, look at you."

Tereasa stood and looked to the team one leader. "Get them the fuck out of here! Oh, this one goes back to Georgia. Those with me will take him," she said.

Then turned and gave instructions to the ones who'd come with her. When she finished, she turned to Gina.

"Oh, and Ms. Williamson. When we get back, clean out your locker. You're being reassigned."

"What? Reassigned?" Gina asked vexedly.

"Yeah, I can't have agents on my team who are disloyal and won't follow my orders. You're being moved to the Midwestern division," Tereasa told her.

Then added. "A word of advice... I don't know who your senior agent will be but learn how to roll with the punches. You don't question those who are over you. That's career suicide."

Tereasa watched as her head dropped in shame. "Hey, I didn't get you fired. I just can't work with you. See, I'm the Queen Bitch on the East Coast." With that said, she turned and walked off. Gina stood there looking stupid. And the sad part was, she knew better from the start. She'd seen just how much power this bitch had the first day she met her.

Chapter Sixteen
Memphis, Tennessee

Chalice sat inside of the Waffle House along with B'Nice John John and Black Smoke, eating. They'd been in Memphis for two days now. He'd already sent a message that he wanted to meet this King G, but he hadn't heard anything yet. They'd already spoken with the guys in South and North Carolina. He still had to go up to Virginia, but first, he needed to meet this guy. This King Gangsta, as he was called.

"Heads up," Black Smoke said.

He nodded his head towards the entourage of cars that all pulled into the parking lot. There were a variety of cars from the old school box Chevy to the new Cadillac Fleetwood and Coupe. They watched as a guy shorter than all four of them stepped out of the new model black Fleetwood that had the gangster whitewalls on it. The guy wore gold frame glasses and had his hair in locks. they watched as a group of them formed up around him and proceeded to enter the Waffle House.

Chalice went back to eating as if nothing was happening. It wasn't long before they entered. Black Smoke was facing the door, so he saw when one of them tapped the guy on the shoulder and pointed towards them. Then they all turn and walked over to the table.

"Pardon me, which one of you guys put the word in the streets that you were looking for King G?"

Chalice turned his head and looked up at the guy that stood over his table.

"And which one of you is King G?" he asked.

But he already knew because there were pictures that came with the profiles.

"That depends on why you're looking for him," King G

said.

Chalice sat in thought a moment. From the looks of it, this guy had the team. But did he have the type of mind that he was looking for?

"Look, I've got a business proposition for you..." Chalice looked back to Black Smoke. Both he and John John were seated on the other side of the table. Chalice gave them both a nod. The two of them stood and moved to the next table. Chalice looked back to this guy.

"Bring one of your people and have a seat." Chalice glanced around at the rest of them. "I doubt if you're going to need all of them."

He waited and watched as King G spoke to his people. After their brief interaction, most of them turned and left out. He and three others stayed. King G took a seat across from Chalice and they began to talk about business.

*****

Joker walked through the restaurant and spoke with a few of the customers here and there. This restaurant wasn't as exclusive as the one he'd owned in Miami, but there were still a lot of benefits to it. Here he catered to all of the doctors, lawyers, bankers, and those of that caliber who worked alongside Chalice's Black Family which was a plus. It allowed him the opportunity to get to know that inner circle better because he still had a lot of money overseas in several bank accounts. Through the banker, he was currently in the process of purchasing at least three more buildings. Although, he wasn't sure yet of what type of business he would use them for. Nevertheless, it was a good way for him to establish roots in Augusta. His Uncle Diego said that he may have to relocate his family soon. Knowing now that his brother was the one behind what happened to Joker, Diego knew that Hector held ill feelings towards him too because he maintained a connection to Joker. He'd explained that his brother was a very vindictive person, so he was looking for someplace to move.

Joker also remembered that Diego said should Hector find out that he was in dealings with his in-laws, there would be conflict. Diego's wife was a great-niece to Valentino Ramirez, who wasn't a favorite of the other Cartel families. Should that happen, then Diego would also need a place of refuge in the States.

*****

With both Cory and Mustafa out of the way, it left a serious void in the streets. No one knew what happened to Cory, but word about Mustafa hit the streets hard. "What it is, Po' Bitch?" Baby Nick asked as he exited his C-Class Benz Sedan, having just pulled up into one of the parking lot circles in Barton Village where Pocket Change ran his hustle.

Pocket Change looked up from counting the hand full of bills he held. Baby Nick seemed to have stepped his game up considerably since word hit that Mustafa got popped. Pocket Change took in the Pelle Pelle jeans, Sean John shirt with the latest Air Forces.

"Yeah, I see you. I see you, Thug." He smiled.

Baby Nick had been the one left holding the last twenty-five keys Mustafa had left.

"What? This?" Baby Nick held his arms up and looked down at himself. "This ain't shit, thug. Just a few gents I picked up," he said.

Baby Nick had given both Pocket Change and Rico Lokeys a piece. But he'd explained that the reup would depend on how much they had when he found a plug to buy from.

"Yeah, I hear you, thug." Pocket Change laughed. "You hear anything from that Po' Bitch yet?"

"Yeah," Baby Nick said. "I just gave Latoria thirty stacks for the lawyer and I put ten on his books. He good though."

That was another reason Baby Nick kept thirteen keys. He knew that he was going to keep Mustafa straight and pay for the lawyer.

"I still can't believe the bitch kept her job too. That nigga got to be sitting good up in there," Pocket Change said.

The Feds were using a few cells in Phinizy Road to house their criminals and Latoria worked at the jail. That made it easier for Mustafa to get the phone and weed that Baby Nick sent him.

"Not really... She wasn't with him when they picked him and his plug up. She was still at the hotel, so they didn't connect her to the bust." Baby Nick told him. Because Latoria had already explained it to him.

"Yeah... Well, what the Lawyer talkin 'bout?" Pocket Change asked as he reshuffled the bills in his hand.

"Sheeeit.... They say thug looking at twenty, fed time. They was really after the plug though," Baby Nick said.

What Baby Nick didn't tell him was that Latoria had been shooting at him and he was seriously thinking about tapping that ass.

"But look, thug.... I stopped by to tell you that I might have us a plug," Baby Nick said.

"What, you need a nigga to ride down wit' you?"

"Nahhh..." Baby Nick drug the word out. "I actually pulled up on that nigga Paris. You know thug got some good prices."

Baby Nick stopped talking when he noticed the sour look

that came across Pocket Change's face.

"I dunno, thug," Pocket Change said. "You know them niggaz is the enemy. What you think Mustafa gon' say about us buying from them?"

"Shit thug, what can he say?" Baby Nick asked.

"Either a nigga keep his feet wet out here or he goes out of business," he continued. "And I'm not about to be on the road trying to traffic shit. Not when these niggaz got good prices right here. I'ma buy from 'em. If y'all don't wanna get down, then that's on y'all."

With that said, Baby Nick left it alone. At the end of the day, it wasn't him who had beef with this nigga Paris. That was some of Mustafa's shit and he wasn't about to lose money thinking like a petty nigga. That just didn't make sense.

Chapter Seventeen
Six Months Later

For the fourth time in five months, the South American-North American Council came together to meet and discuss their problem. Not that it was a new problem. And not that it hadn't already been addressed.

Justina De'Grace sighed as she sat in her seat and listen to the men go around in circles for the fifth time with the same issue.

"We're already losing money," one of the other cartel representatives said. "This guy is crippling the market."

"Yeah, but nobody wants to agree as one about sending Cholos after him," another one added.

Justina knew that would be a bad idea. Going after Chalice would make the Ghost even madder than they were. To prove their point, they'd taken down two other representatives after Franko.

"I'm telling you guys," another representative said. "It's the bitch. She's trying to prove a point."

Justina knew that was the root of the problem. The Ghost had been mad when the other Cartel members wouldn't go for their deal. And with Ramirez in the bed with them, it made the rest of them the enemy. The Ghost still allowed them to move their product into the States, but they'd imposed a weight restriction. Trucks crossing over could only weigh so much. If it was even slightly too heavy, the tax would go up. This was anyone other than Ramirez. Him, they let move as much cocaine as he wanted across which was becoming bad for business.

As a result of running Joker out of Miami, they'd inadvertently redirected the cocaine traffic. Instead of dealers coming to Miami to buy coke, they were starting to go to the small city of Augusta, Georgia.

"We have to do something. We can't continue to sit here and lose money because of this bullshit," someone said.

"I agree," Justina's voice entered the argument. And as it did, all heads and eyes turned to her. She took the time to meet all of the other eyes.

Justina sighed. "I know you're not going to agree. But the more I think about it, the only logical thing to do seems to be to make a deal with Swoop," she said.

She heard a few people curse under their breaths, but she went on to explain.

"Listen... To her, it's just business. The Ghost only wants us to increase our shipments and pay a higher tax. By increasing we make enough to pay their tax, easily."

"Even if we wanted to send more cocaine across, how could our buyers secure as much?" someone asked.

"Yeah, larger amounts also means the price goes down. We were making more money," someone suggested.

"But this guy, Chalice, has changed all of that in less than six months," Justina pointed out. "Already, the price of a kilo is down fifteen grand and likely to go down another fifteen by the end of the year," she outlined.

They all realized that Chalice was getting too much cocaine for them to compete with him. While he steadily dropped the prices, it allowed him to move more and leaving them stuck with a lot of cocaine and fewer buyers. Rumors had it that buyers were coming from as far as Texas. And with the Ghost on his side, Chalice could guarantee delivery of good product by at least 90%. While all they could guarantee 34 to 40% delivery and half as good as Ramirez product in proof. This meant that every last one of them was losing serious money

"Even if we wanted to accept their deal, they'd only take

it up higher now," someone suggested.

"Maybe not," Justina stated. "I may be able to negotiate a reasonable deal on behalf of every family. But there will be a problem," she said.

"What's the problem?" someone asked.

She knew they weren't going to like this part.

"We'll have to deal with Valentino... And possibly this guy, Chalice," she said.

And sure enough, they cursed for exactly three minutes.

After a short pause, one of the older representatives said, "We'll have to ask our Jefe's."

"However," another older one added. "If they agree, are you sure that you can secure the deal?"

Justina thought about the young black man, Chalice. He was intelligent and proving to be more dangerous than any one of the men seated at the table. And yet, even that didn't strike fear in her. Instead, she was experiencing the opposite. Her vagina seemed to contract and moisten at the mere thought of her sitting across from the table with him to discuss business. Justina hadn't felt this way in some time. She was surprised to feel it now. She cleared her throat.

"I believe that there's a great chance that I can convince them," she said. "All I'll need is permission from all of the families."

"In that case, give us seventy-two hours. We'll have a decision by then."

Unfortunately, this meant that she would have to wait. Justina began to mentally make plans for her trip back to Augusta. The private investigator had included detailed instructions on how to best contact Chalice. She would have to go through the wife. That was the only way that he would conduct business.

And right now, they seriously needed to establish some

type of business relationship. That or be run out of business. As she stood to leave, Justina was also contemplating another type of relationship being established.

Chapter Eighteen

Chalice stood in front of the Range Rover wearing the two-piece suit and the extended trench coat. The headlights were on and casting shadows. There were four shadows. Along with him, there were the other three men who stood with him. To his immediate right stood Paris, while on his left, stood Black Smoke and Diamond. All of them were pretty much dressed the same. With it being the middle of November, the weather was pretty cold, and the wind was blowing some.

Neither one of them spoke as they stood there and watched as the eighteen-wheel semi pulled onto the dirt road. The truck was being followed by a black Avalanche pick up. They watched as the truck came to a complete stop with its high beams still on. None of them made a move to shield their eyes from the brighter light. Instead, they waited and watched as the large Mexican exited the truck, leaving it running. The Mexican then walked over to them.

"Senior Chalice..." He pushed his hand out.

Chalice took the man's hand.

"Que unda, Puppet. Todo bien?" Chalice asked.

"Si.... mula en la banco." Puppet smiled.

"Good. Then tell Valentino I send my best." Chalice turned to Paris. "Get the man his money, bruh."

Paris walked to the back of the Range Rover along with Diamond and they removed four large duffle bags. Which they brought around to the front and sat in front of Puppet. The passenger door of the Avalanche opened and another large Mexican stepped out. He walked up to stand next to Puppet.

"Que unda, Scrappy," Chalice said.

Scrappy, who was a man of few words, gave Chalice a smile and a head nod. He bent and picked up two of the bags. Puppet grabbed the other two.

"Alright then carnalito," Puppet said. "We have a long ride back to Texas. We'll see you on the next shipment."

Chalice watched as the two Mexicans walked back to the Avalanche and entered it. The truck backed up and turned around.

"Diamond, you ride with Paris. Me and Black Smoke have some other things to look into," Chalice said. Then he looked to Paris. "Once y'all unload everything and put it in storage, take the truck to the truck yard."

Since they were receiving these shipments by trucks, Paris, John John, and Que all had their CDL's now. The trucks themselves were already theirs. Having been driven to Texas empty and returned with the delivery inside. The system itself was Ramirez's set up. No one other than them knew how or when the cocaine was delivered. Chalice didn't tell them until an hour away from the pickup.

*****

For some reason, Pocket Change still wasn't feeling the move. He was starting to have bad vibes about this situation between Baby Nick and Latoria. Pocket Change sat in his Mustang parked further up the street from where Latoria lived. He watched as Baby Nick sat on the hood of his Benz and held a conversation with Latoria, who stood on the sidewalk looking like a ghetto diva. From just watching the two, he could see that they weren't talking about Mustafa. The conversation looked much more personal. Pocket Change couldn't explain why it bothered him other than the fact that he kinda had a thing for Latoria himself, but he didn't feel like he was hating.

*****

"So, you expect me to believe, ain't no nigga pulled up and tried to get at you since ole boy been gone?" Baby Nick asked.

He watched as Latoria stood there and shuffled from one foot to another like a nervous virgin. What got him was the fact that she was five years older than him, but at the moment she was acting like he was older.

"You already know he had the boo on these niggaz out here." She laughed like a little girl.

"Got you thinking you all of that too, huh?" He smiled.

He watched as she sucked her teeth.

"What you tryna say then?" she asked.

Baby Nick looked her up and down. She was rocking Ferragamo jeans, a Coogi sweater, and her chunky open-toe Gucci heels. *She was definitely fly,* he thought.

"Nah, I'm just saying one of these niggaz should have been at you by now."

"You said that like you would have," she said.

"Well... I mean if a nigga figured he had a real shot at it, maybe I would have," he said.

"And you wouldn't have been worried about Mustafa?" she inquired.

He tilted his head like he was thinking about it.

"I mean... You a grown woman... Shit, you can fuck with whoever you wanna fuck wit', right?" he asked.

"Yeah, but he was yo' boy and all," Latoria said.

They both fell silent in thought for a moment. Then Baby Nick said.

"You know what... Fuck that, you wanna kick it?"

"Maybe." Latoria smiled. "We'll see how things play out."

But the decision had already been made.

*****

"So how you gon' handle this thing with Baby Nick?" Diamond asked as he and Paris sat inside the Huddle House eating.

"What you mean?" Paris said around a mouthful of food.

"I'm just asking cause I sort of like the lil nigga. I remember you saying something about the nigga was on the opposing team," Diamond explained.

"Yeah, that nigga Mustafa brought him into the game. But shit, that nigga outta the picture now," Paris said.

Seeing as it wasn't a secret with what happened to Mustafa. It had been the talk for at least two weeks when it went down.

"Besides..." Paris continued. "The lil nigga got his shit together. He sort of reminds me of myself when I was nineteen." Which wasn't actually a long time ago. Paris was only twenty-six now. When he was nineteen, they were horsemen and out to take over all of Augusta. Now they pretty much ran 80% of all street activities.

"We gon' watch the lil nigga," Paris said. "Let him get his hustle on and see where it takes him," he further explained

When Baby Nick first pushed up on him, he thought that it might've been a setup. But the more he talked to the younger man, the more he saw his ambition. Baby Nick pretty much wanted what Mustafa had had.

"What made you notice him too?" Paris asked.

"The way the lil nigga keeps talking 'bout making some extra bands. He's talking like he's saving up for a rainy day or something like it," Diamond said.

Falling deep into his thoughts, Paris remembered that look inside of Baby Nick's eyes. It was the look of a man that believed in himself. The look of a guy that didn't wait for it to fall out of the sky and they could both sense the same hunger. That's what they both saw inside of Baby Nick. Not greed, hate, lust, or envy. It was determination. Both the will and the desire to see better, be better by doing better. Neither one of them felt like Baby Nick was the enemy, which was why Paris agreed to give him a plug.

"Well, we gon' see what he does when I give him this drop. See if he stands up," Paris said.

He went on to finish eating his food. Diamond knew they weren't fucking with Baby Nick's whole crew. But also, that Baby Nick would have to step his game up with them. Not even Mustafa was getting the amount of product that they would be giving him and that was because of the amount of cocaine they were now getting.

Chapter Nineteen

"Listen..." Felipe looked across the table into the eyes of the other man. Although he was a twin, he didn't exactly look like his brother. "My father is against the whole thing, but he won't say it aloud because everyone else seems to be with it," he explained.

"And your cousin..." He continued. "We don't think she knows what she's doing. We think she's losing her touch."

"Are you willing to say that to her face?" Emanuel De' Grace asked, showing his teeth with a sinister smile on his face.

This meeting was being held inside of a popular Miami restaurant, which at the moment wasn't that crowded.

"Come on... We all know how unstable she can be," Felipe said. Then continued. "My father's just trying to avoid making a bad business decision. That's why I asked to see you. This thing with the black guy, it's not a good thing."

"But the others have already agreed to it. What do you expect me to do about it?" Emanuel asked.

Felipe sighed heavily. He knew Emanuel was the weaker of the two. However, Hector said to see if they could avoid having to enter into business with these people who were associated with his Uncle Joker, and somehow remove this guy Chalice. Felipe thought it would be best to give someone in the De'Grace family a heads up about their next move.

"Look, we have a plan," Felipe said. "This plan involves us sending some people who won't be afraid to go after this guy. We just wanted to give your people the heads up."

"Justina has already left to meet up with this guy and you know nothing can happen to her," Emmanuel stated.

Felipe rolled his eyes.

"Do you think we're stupid? No harm will come to your

cocaine Queen. We just need this situation with Joker to be taken care of once and for all," Felipe said.

What he hadn't said was that his father, Hector Giovani, really wasn't happy with the way that the De'Grace family had attempted to remove Joker only to make him more powerful. Hector was under the impression that it was Joker who was really behind these dealings with Valentino Ramirez. And he wasn't happy about the other families bowing down the way they were about to.

*****

"What's on your mind?" Erica asked as she drove the white SLS-AMG Convertible Coupe. Having just gotten the car a few weeks ago. She brought the car because Tereasa said that she would look good driving something sleek and sexy.

"Just thinking," Chalice told her from the passenger seat.

"Are you sure it's a good idea to do business with these people? This woman is very dangerous," he told her.

They were on their way to a meeting with Justina De'Grace at a five-star restaurant, which was why they were both dressed to impress. She, in an expensive Versace dress, while he wore an Armani suit.

"Tereasa has told me all about the woman," Erica stated as she drove. "She also said this woman was an important piece to the game her people were playing with the cartel and that we should make this deal work. By any means."

She'd already explained once, so he knew what they were supposed to do at this meeting. Chalice really didn't have a problem doing business with Justina De'Grace. He could do business with anybody as long as they had an understanding. But there was just something about this woman they were about to meet with, and he couldn't place his finger on it.

*****

They were shown to the table where the elegantly Justina De'Grace sat. Upon reaching the table Justina stood to greet them. Chalice's eyes scanned her body in the expensive Ferragamo evening gown she wore. The woman was fine. He didn't think that Justina had any children because her hips were still kind of narrow for a South American woman. Her waistline was also small, her breast sat up high and proud. The golden-brown tint of her skin looked like she'd just left a Brazilian beach getting an all-over tan.

"Mrs. Scurry, it's so nice to finally meet the legend in the flesh." Justina shook hands with Erica. "I've heard so much of your years in Miami."

"Older years, I assume. But please, call me Erica."

Justina then turned her attention to Chalice.

"Chalice, it's nice to see you again, and under uh...better circumstances," she stated.

Chalice simply smiled. He watched as they sat, and Justina's focus went back to Erica. It was almost as if he wasn't even sitting there, so he kept quiet.

"So, what exactly are the other families trying to do?"

"One moment." Justina raised her hand and waved the waiter over.

They ordered their meal and a nice bottle of Chardonnay. When the waiter left, she said, "Well, it seems your husband has us all in an uh....unique situation," Justina began. "Never in my lifetime have I seen or heard of someone moving the way that he does. In just under a year's time since it became known that you were working with these Ghost, cocaine prices have dropped greatly and become plentiful."

"It's a marketing strategy," Chalice put in. "I receive

enough product that I can do that and still make more money."

"It would seem," Justina commented. Before she could say more, their food came, so all conversation stopped.

Being an older, experienced woman, who specialized in knowing and recognizing lust, Erica could see the way that this woman watched Chalice. She had lust all in her eyes, but she didn't think that Chalice saw it.

After the waiter left Erica said, "You mentioned that you were here to make a deal on behalf of the entire cartel structure."

"We would like to amend our dealings with Tereasa Swoop, the Ghost's spokesperson." Justina began. "A while back she came to us with terms that we couldn't agree to at that time, but now it seems that we may not have a choice. The families would like to make a deal where we don't lose too much," she expressed.

"Okay... So why reach out to me? Why didn't you contact Ms. Swoop?" Erica asked.

"When last the families spoke with her, she was trying to arrest all of the North American representatives," Justina explained as they ate. "We, uh...." She glanced up and looked directly at Erica. "We need a middle person. Someone that Swoop would listen to."

If she didn't know any better, Erica thought. She would assume that this woman knew about the inner nature of their relationship with Tereasa. How that could be, Erica wasn't sure, unless they had people watching Chalice's business dealings.

"Alright then, give me an outline of your proposal," Erica told her.

While they talked business, Chalice was trying his best to act nonchalant, especially since Justina's foot somehow seemed to magically begin caressing the calf of his left leg.

The action confirmed what he thought he'd sensed, so his mind wasn't on anything that Erica and Justina said. That was until his name was mentioned.

"I'm pretty sure that Ms. Swoop would consider your deal. However, your people do know that they'll have to do some business with Chalice, right?" Erica stated.

Chalice's eyes came up and met Justina's, who smiled.

"I've extended my hand out to Chalice once before, but now I'm thinking I may need to extend a foot as well."

"Anything is possible," he said.

And for a moment there was a pause as he looked into the South American woman's eyes.

"How about I try to get Ms. Swoop on the phone?" Erica pulled her phone out and pushed her chair back. "I'm sure Chalice wouldn't mind entertaining you for a bit."

He waited until she stepped away from the table.

"I knew you were dangerous, but I didn't think that you were that bold," he said.

Justina smiled across the table.

"You didn't seem to mind," she said. "Do you think that your beautiful wife would want to kill me for being attracted to you?"

"I doubt it." He glanced back to where Erica stood at the far end of the room talking. "Knowing her, she'll want to sample your goods herself."

"Oh. A couple that shares...." Justina smiled as she placed both elbows on the table and leaned forward. "For some reason, just the thought of you makes me wet. I haven't been affected like that by a man in nearly ten years now."

"So, you're telling me..." Chalice paused to lick his lips slowly. "That it's been close to ten years since a man has touched your bottom."

"It's been eight years since I've been with anyone,"

Justina told him as her eyes followed the tip of his tongue. "But I couldn't say anyone has ever reached that deep."

"You don't say." He smiled.

"You sound as if you could reach the bottom yourself," she stated.

"It's possible." He smiled.

"Do you think Erica would let us find out?" she asked.

"I believe I could convince her."

The conversation ended as Erica returned. And he saw that look in her eyes, so he smiled at her.

Chapter Twenty

Yeah, he could tell it had been eight years, Chalice thought as he moved his hips back. Drawing his dick nearly all the way out of her pussy, he had her left leg up over his shoulder while the right one was bent at the knee on the bed. The position gave him a perfect view of his dick as it penetrated her once again slowly.

"Oooohh," Justina moaned out.

Chalice lifted his eyes to look at her face. Her eyes were closed, and her head turned. Both of her hands gripped the bed covers tightly. Her pussy was tight and almost felt as if it fit him perfectly. She wasn't that deep either. That, or he was larger than any man that had ever been inside of her. When Erica finished her call and said that Tereasa would meet with Justina tomorrow, the last thing he thought Justina would expect to happen was for Erica to say she had some other business to attend to. She'd said that he should stay and finish discussing their upcoming business. Erica had then bent to whisper into his ear so that only the three of them could hear her.

"Show her how much we appreciate her business, baby. And don't hold back... I'll see you tomorrow."

She'd looked back to Justina. "You have fun, but don't hurt yourself."

Chalice leaned forward, pressing her leg back and into the bed as he began to pick up the pace. His strokes became longer and deeper. Chalice was doing something to her that he'd done to Teresa. Making a permanent impression upon her vagina. One that said his name should have been a tattoo on both her thighs because they had a whole lot of plans for Ms. De'Grace.

*****

Baby Nick held onto her hips as he dug into her doggy style. Inside his mind, he was thinking of all those times he had thought about fucking Latoria. But that was when she was Mustafa's girl. Now, she was his girl. Oh, she still took Mustafa contraband into the jail. Cigarettes made quite a bit of money on the inside. Baby Nick had explained to her that they didn't want to break the news to the nigga just yet.

He picked up more speed as the sound of their flesh connecting echoed throughout the bedroom. She'd asked him to move in right after the first time they fucked, but Baby Nick had told her that he'd have to do something about this nigga Pocket Change first. Baby Nick didn't like the slick shit this nigga was saying. And he knew that if Mustafa got some proof that he was fucking Latoria, the nigga could send some smoke his way. This nigga, Pocket Change, had to go.

It was a good thing he was meeting up with this nigga, Paris, tomorrow. If that shit went right, then he could give a fuck about Mustafa. But for the moment, he concentrated on blowing Latoria's back out and making her his permanent bitch."

*****

B'Nice stepped off the elevator and rushed to the desk. The nurse sitting behind it looked up.

"Yes.... May I help you?"

"My girlfriend is in labor. Could you tell me where I can find her?" he asked.

"Delivery is down the end of this hall. The nurse at that desk will be able to tell you where she is."

He turned and headed that way. In the end, he stepped into the room while they were preparing Shae. B'Nice moved over to the bed and grabbed her hand.

"How you doing, baby?" He smiled.

"Muthafucka.... This shit is not funny," she stressed between breaths as she breathed in and out.

"Yeah, I know Ma... But you sho' looking sexy right now," he said because it looked like she'd just had her hair done. And it was one of those expensive curly-type of styles.

"You see Pumpkin?" she asked. "She and Paris brought me here. They should be in the waiting room," she said.

"Nah, I ain't seen em, but I'll check on them later. Right now, it's all about you, baby," he told her,

"You see... That right there is how we got here in the first place." She stopped to breathe. "All of yo' sweet-talking and shit. "Nigga we ain't doing this again."

B'Nice smiled. "Of course, we are Ma. Remember, I told you that I wanted a boy and a girl."

"Nigga..." Her words fell short because of another contraction, but B'Nice wasn't paying her protest any attention. Instead, he was planning the future for his forthcoming child.

*****

Paris hadn't really been into drinking coffee until he started hanging with Diamond. Now as he sat next to Pumpkin inside of the waiting room. He sipped on the cup of straight black coffee. Pumpkin had her phone out and was texting people, so she was all off into her phone. Paris was thinking about the next move he was about to make. Having made the decision to put Baby Nick on they just had to do something about the other two niggaz. Baby Nick said that both Pocket Change and Rico were still loyal to Mustafa. And that they would cause problems as soon as word got out that he was doing business with the Black Family. Baby Nick said that Mustafa could still be a problem even from inside, which was why Paris had put some other plans into motion. Mustafa would be taken care of, but these two niggaz needed to be dealt with now.

*****

"You going to count first, or should I?" Cathy asked.

"I've got it." The other officer grasped the flashlight and stepped out of the control booth. She waited for Cathy to open the door so that she could step inside.

It was after lockdown, so all of the guys were locked in their cells. Which meant that all she had to do was walk around and count how many men were in each cell. Something she did with ease. Phinizy Road was the new jail and getting the job was pretty easy. She counted all of the rooms on one side then counted the other. When she reached this one particular room, she wasn't surprised to see the older, brown-skinned guy standing at the door. He always did that when she made rounds. Just like she wasn't surprised when he showed her his cell phone. This guy had been trying to talk to her since she started. And part of his game was trying to corrupt her.

Drucilla smiled at him showing off her dimples. "Betta be careful what you ask for. You might not be able to handle it," she said and continued with her count.

Mustafa watched as the new chocolate-covered dime piece moved in. *Yeah....* He thought. *I can damn sure handle whatever she had to give.*

He turned and walked back to his bed. He didn't have a roommate because the feds had him there for holding. Mustafa looked back to the screenshot of Baby Nick and Latoria talking. She was sitting on the hood of her car as he stood between her legs. Pocket Change had taken the picture earlier, having been sitting in a car up the street from where she lived.

He'd also mentioned this nigga, Baby Nick, was talking about buying work from the nigga Paris. Not that he blamed the nigga for trying to stay on his feet, but... "This nigga gon' fuck my bitch and fuck wit' my enemy."

That shit was just too disrespectful, which was why he had Pocket Change following the nigga. As soon as he got the work, he and Rico were to hit the nigga. They are going to take the work and kill him. Pocket Change wanted to kill Latoria too, but Mustafa told him that would be stupid. The bitch was still useful. She brought his shit in for him. And until he found another mule, he needed her. He didn't know how long the FEDS would have him there. Hopefully, he was about to pull this new bitch, Ms. Cortez. *Yeah.* He smiled. *I'ma definitely get that bitch.*

Trai'Quan

Chapter Twenty-One

Justina knew that the rest of the families wouldn't like the terms of the deal she'd worked out with Tereasa Swoop, but there wasn't much that could be done about it. They would be given the chance to make more money than they had been making prior to this, with less risk to those who were higher up. In other words, none of them would have to fear the Ghost coming after them, but their buyers weren't given the same protection. They were still targets for the DEA and U.S. Customs, but she thought about the way Chalice explained it. If they chose their buyers based upon their ability to think and not based upon how much money they had, then it wouldn't be a problem. They needed *thinkers*, not hustlers.

Justina pulled into the driveway of her family's house. She exited the Lexus ISC Convertible sedan and walked towards the house. She'd seen both of her cousins' cars also parked out front, so she knew they were there. She found both of them in the study with drinks in hand.

"Well, I see you're in good health," Emanuel stated as she walked over to the bar and made a drink for herself.

"And. Why wouldn't I be?" she asked.

"Considering the fact that some of the families nearly placed a hit on you," Fernando added.

She looked back to the both of them.

"it's a good thing you're no longer in the presence of the people Joker associates with," Emanuel said, which caught her attention fully.

"And why is that?" she asked.

"Because Hector Giovani has placed a contract on not only Joker, but the guy that's been causing all of these problems. I think his name is Chalice."

"Hector wouldn't be so stupid," Justina proclaimed. "That

would be the worst thing that he could do. This guy is under the protection of the Ghost. Tereasa Swoop would be highly offended if someone attempted to kill him."

She watched as Emanuel laughed after she stopped talking. It was as if he found something highly amusing.

"Did I say something funny?" she asked.

"It's just that you assume it's a regular contract," Emanuel stated. "Felipe told me personally that Hector is sending some of his best Sicario. He's spent good money to have these people eliminated. And I don't think he's worried about what the Ghost will have to say about it."

Justina thought over what was said. And she hadn't even realized that her heart was beating faster. Because her thoughts were of Chalice. She had to warn him. But she couldn't let these two fools know. They seem to be doing a lot of socializing with Felipe.

*****

Having been at the gym for the past hour. Chalice finished his work out and snatched up his towel. Usually, he put in thirty minutes every Monday, Wednesday, and Friday. That was enough to keep him in shape. But for some reason, today he seemed to have a lot of extra energy. When he started, he'd been thinking to do just thirty minutes, but that turned into an hour. And he had to consciously stop then. Because he still felt like he could go harder.

"Maybe I'm just getting old," he mumbled to himself as he headed for the showers.

He didn't see any other way to explain it. When men grew older, they tend to fight time. As if they could turn back the hands of time or make them stop altogether.

Chalice undressed and stepped under the shower spray. He

would be thirty in a few months. And while out loud it didn't sound old. To him, thirty felt old. Chalice also thought about all he'd done over the past seven-plus years. They'd actually accomplished a lot. More than he would have thought. He finished showering then stepped out. Using the towel that he was in the process of drying himself when he thought he heard a noise.

"What the fuck was that?"

Chalice knew there wasn't anyone else at the gym. He liked to work out alone. He wrapped the towel around his waist and went to remove the H&K P-20 that Tereasa had given him. As he made his way to the door of the shower area, he jacked a bullet into the chamber. Somewhere inside of his mind there seem to exist an echo. A reminder of when he was shot and placed in a coma. Chalice stepped into the gym and stood still. The only thing he moved were his eyes. He looked around carefully. Having known the gym like the back of his hand, nothing seemed out of order.

And just as that thought came, it was as if his spider senses started tingling. Over the years he'd learned to not question or second guess the feeling. Chalice stepped to his left quickly. And as soon as his shoulder bumped into the snack machine, he felt the breeze as the led pipe sailed through the air right where his head had just been a second ago. Chalice turned so that he could get a shot off, but as soon as he saw the rough-looking South American with the thick mustache, his spider senses tingled again. He rolled around the machine just as another piece of metal slammed into it. Chalice saw that there were two of them. And before he could get a shot off, the first guy knocked the gun from his hand. And instinct took over after that. Chalice brought his right foot up and kicked the guy with the pipe. He fell to the side but caught himself. Chalice couldn't follow through because the second man took a swing with the baseball bat he held. He was able to dodge the bat and then grab it. Chalice jerked and pulled the man off balance. In doing so, he twisted him so that the man with the pipe's next swing hit him in the shoulder.

"AAAH!" he cried out.

Chalice felt his grip on the bat loosen and it was just enough for him to pull it out of the man's hand. Now he had the bat. Chalice flipped it so that he now held it the right way. He drew back and swung, hitting the empty-handed man in the head, which sent him to the floor. Chalice then turned to meet the man with the led pipe in full swing with the bat. He then kicked the man holding the pipe backwards. The man stumbled and fell. At that point Chalice's eyes landed on the gun. He tossed the bat and bent to pick it up.

BOOOOM...BOOOOOM...BOOOM...

Chalice placed all three shots at center mass directly in the man's chest. He turned to the unconscious one.

BOOOOM...BOOOM...

A double-tap, both shots to the head. And as soon as things quiet down, Chalice heard his phone ring. He looked down at both dead men and went to his bag to get his phone. When he looked at it, he saw that it was Justina's number.

"Yeah?" he answered.

"Where are you? Are you safe?" she asked.

"I'm at the gym. And I'm alright now. Why? What made you ask that?" He was curious. Seeing as the men themselves were South American.

"I just found out that Hector Giovani and his son, Felipe, put a contract on you and Joker. They're sending Sicario after you. Mexican killers," she explained.

Chalice looked back to where the two bodies lay. He'd heard of these Sicario. And from just the fight they'd had, he didn't think that these were the best they had.

"Well, I just killed two of them. But I'm thinking there might be some more," he said.

"You've killed two... By yourself?" She seemed surprised.

"Yeah, but I don't think these were their best. Look, I need to get dressed and call Joker. But thanks for the heads up," he said.

"I just hope what Hector has done doesn't hurt our deal. I've checked. He's acted alone in this," she explained.

"Then the rest of you have nothing to worry about. Just leave Hector and Felipe to me. I'll call you once we've straightened things up here." He ended the call.

Chalice thought about the end of the movie Scarface. *If these people were serious, then it was going down big in the A-U-G.*

Trai'Quan

Chapter Twenty-Two

Joker was awakened by the ringing of the phone. When he reached for it, he didn't even look at the number.

"Hello," he spoke.

"Two of your grandfather's Sicario just tried to kill me," Chalice's voice said. "Word is, he's sent them after me and you. So, I'd suggest you send La'Donna to my house and Erica will make sure she's alright. You get Black Smoke, Que, and John John and be ready for whatever."

"What about you? What are you going to do?" Joker asked.

"What I should have done from the start." The phone went dead.

Joker sat there thinking for a minute before he woke La'Donna and explained the situation. While she dressed, he called Black Smoke and told him to come to the house. He didn't know what Chalice was up to, but killing two Sicario wasn't a small issue. Joker knew about the situation Chalice had going on with the Ghost and the other cartel families. Chalice had actually come to him for advice and he'd told him the best way to go about it. Apparently, his grandfather wasn't trying to do business that way. Joker had told Chalice that his grandfather would be a problem. Even if the other families went along with it. His grandfather was a stubborn old man who had little respect for people with darker skin, so he knew the negotiations wouldn't work with Chalice to be sitting at the head of the table. But then again, Joker didn't exactly know what Chalice was really capable of.

*****

When Chalice stepped off the elevator and entered the

waiting room, he found both Paris and B'Nice talking. They both looked up when they saw him.

"So, what did baby girl have, a boy or girl?" Chalice asked.

"I've got a daughter," B'Nice said proudly. "We named her Leshay."

"Congratulations!" Chalice hugged him and then stepped back.

"Ok... So y'all ready to see about this business?"

Over the phone, Chalice had given them a brief outline of what was going on.

"You said something about a road trip," Paris said.

Chalice glanced around to make sure no one could hear his words. And since they were standing in front of the window, he was looking down into the parking lot.

"When I leave here, you two will follow me in your own rides. There are two cars following me. I don't know how many people are in each one. Two Chrysler Sedans, same make and model. We need to dead everybody in both of them before we make this drive to Miami," Chalice explained.

"A'ight. And once we reach Miami?" B'Nice asked.

Chalice was silent for a moment.

"We take out the entire Giovani stateside family. Their time in America has expired," Chalice said.

"A'ight. We're ready when you're ready, bruh. But I did have a small problem I needed to solve," Paris stated.

"It shouldn't take us long to handle these muthafuckaz in the Chryslers. Can your problem be solved in the next six hours?" Chalice asked.

"Yeah, it's a small matter really," Paris told him as he dug into his pocket and pulled out his phone.

Over the years, both Paris and B'Nice had become his extension. Most of the work he put in and wasn't done with

Erica, it was done with them. Especially when she'd been pregnant with Quintessa. At that point, he'd officially placed her in retirement from all street activity. But he knew that he could depend on both of them.

*****

"Are you sure this is the guy?" one of the Sicario asked.

"I'm sure," the one sitting behind the steering wheel said. They watched as Chalice exited the hospital and walked over to his black Range Rover 4.6 HSE. They were so focused on Chalice that they didn't see the other two come out.

"This is the guy that took out Marco and Ricardo," the one in the passenger seat said. "I don't get it. This guy looks like a businessman, not a killer."

"Don't underestimate these people. That could be fatal," the one behind the wheel pointed out.

He started the car as soon as Chalice opened his door and entered the SUV. They pulled out of the parking lot following him, while the second Chrysler fell in behind them. None of them knew anything about the city of Augusta, so they had no idea where this guy was going. But it didn't matter anyway. As soon as they had him under the right circumstances, they would take him out and then head back to Mexico.

*****

Chalice crossed the bridge going into South Carolina. As he did, he looked up into the rearview and saw that the two cars were right there.

"Fuckin armatures," he mumbled.

Because it didn't seem like they were trying to be inconspicuous at all as if they didn't care if he noticed the cars following him. Chalice made it a point to pull the cars following him into one of the gas stations and right up next to the pumps. He really needed to know how many men were in each car. And sure enough, they both pulled in behind him. Chalice exited the truck and pushed the gas pump into the tank, then he turned and walked to the store. He saw Paris' black Denali and B'Nice's black Escalade as they rode by slowly.

Inside the store, he grabbed a Juicy Juice, a pack of salted peanuts, and some gum. He stepped up to the counter and paid for his items while keeping an eye on the cars outside. Only one man from each car got out and came inside. One got out and pretended to pump gas. Chalice didn't even acknowledge the men as he walked back outside and stood next to his truck. It seemed as if he was waiting while the gas was being pumped, but it wasn't long before his phone buzzed. He removed it and read the message.

"We're ready... It's your play."

Chalice polished off the peanuts, turned up the Juicy Juice, then tossed both empty containers into the wastebasket. He removed the gas pump, replaced the cap on the gas tank, and re-entered his truck. He knew that when it went down, it would go down fast and hard. So, he left the gas station and made his way to Highway 278 which was where it would be going down. Highway 278 was a long stretch, and it went all the way to the bottom of South Carolina. Most of it was dark because of all the trees and no highway street lights, but Chalice knew the highway too well.

*****

After about ten minutes on the road, the guy in the passenger seat glanced around, then said, "You know... This might just be the best place to get him before we come back to a lighted area."

The driver was just about to agree when he saw the brake lights on the SUV flash, and then the hazard lights were put on as the Range Rover pulled over to the side of the road.

"Looks like something is wrong with his truck," the driver said as he slowed down. He looked over to his friend. "Let's offer the young man our help."

They both touched their guns and smiled. In the car behind them, they had four foot soldiers, so they knew that their backs were covered. They stopped ten feet away from the Range Rover where the driver also pulled over to the side of the road. Their target had stepped out of the truck and was looking at the front tires, so they both stepped out of their car and began to approach him.

"Hey... I just saw you at the store, Amigo. What, you have a flat tire? You need some help?" he asked. Just before the target spoke, they all heard the screech of a vehicle's tires. They turned to look and saw the dark red minivan pull up beside the car their foot soldiers were inside of that was parked to the side of the highway. The side door slid open and they watched as Paris opened up with the Army issued fully adjusted Robar SR-21. This was a Remington 700 Action AR-15 with an extended thirty-round magazine.

The two killers stood there in shock as they watched Paris unload the entire clip into the car. By the time reality set in and they reached for their guns, it was already too late.

"Yeah... I could use some help," Chalice spoke.

And then the Ithaca Mag 10 Shotgun came to life in his hands. The shotgun only came equipped with three shots, but his had been fitted for two extras. With the shotgun and at this distance, Chalice only needed two shots and they both sounded like a thunderstorm.

BOOOM!

The driver was nearly blown in half.

BOOOM!

His friends' entire left side of his body was blown away.

Chalice looked up as B'Nice eased the minivan closer.

"I've got two local muthafuckaz I need to dead, then we can head south," Paris stated.

B'Nice looked across at the smoking shotgun that Chalice still held. The gun looked and sounded like a cannon.

"Shit... You got anything left in that muthafucka?" he asked.

Chalice smiled. "Three more shells," he said.

"Well, fuck it then." B'Nice smiled. "Let's go wake up the dead. That bitch will damn sure do it."

They all laughed.

Chapter Twenty-Three

"Yo... Yo... Hold the fuck up sun." Que said as John John rounded the curve onto Joker's street. As they came into the sight of the house, Que also took notice of the dark grey sedan that was parked a little further up the street.

"Man, you think that's them?" John John asked as he slowed the midnight blue SRT Hellcat down.

John John loved the car because it sounded like an airplane that was about to take off. And when he really punched it, the bitch sounded like a space shuttle going into lift-off. That's how loud the car really was.

"The one people I know it ain't..." Que said. "Is the Alphabet team. Them muthafuckaz work for Ms. Swoop now and she fucks wit' us, so it gotta be them."

The more John John thought about it, the more sense it made. Tereasa Swoop was actually their boss now. They technically worked for her and she'd explained that there would be no problems with the FBI, DEA, or ATF because they would all have to run it by her before they made any type of move concerning the Black Family.

As John John eased past the Sedan slowly, they could easily make out the two men sitting low in the seats, trying to make it look like no one was inside.

"Yo sun... Find somewhere to pull up," Que said, and John John continued driving until they were on the next street over.

He pulled into Cujo and Pam's driveway and parked. They both pulled out their guns. Que, a .45 SP brand Tanus with a laser beam mounted on top. And John John had a black Glock .40, it also had a laser beam on it.

*****

"What the hell are you looking at?" Pam asked.

It was late and she'd heard Cujo leave the bed, so she got up to follow him being nosey. She found him standing at the window in the front room holding the Phillips & Rodgers Model .47 'Medusa' in his hand. He stood firm, looking like he were about to kill King Kong.

"That's John John's loud ass Challenger out there," Cujo said back over his shoulder. "Him and Que just got out with their guns. They went through the yard of that empty house across the street," he explained.

"What do you think is going on?" Pam asked.

"I don't know... But I'm going out there to make sure it ain't nothing crazy," he said.

"Nigga... Ain't you too old for that shit? Let them young niggaz handle it," Pam stated.

She watched, and for a second, it seemed like Cujo would ignore the fact that Chalice's team had been keeping their neighborhood safe. Whatever it was that Que and John John were up to, nine times out of ten, it was something her son told them to do.

"Yeah... You right." Cujo's shoulders slumped.

Pam knew that he was no longer in the streets like that, especially after they'd had Janiece, their six-year-old daughter. Cujo wasn't allowed to do anymore thuggin in the streets.

*****

"You think they see us, homes?" the killer behind the wheel asked. He was nervous and jumpy since the loud muscle car drove by.

"Nah... It was probably some teenagers or something," the other killer said.

The first killer looked across the street to the house. They'd been sitting out front for about fifteen minutes now and the lights inside the house had been out before they pulled up.

"Do you think someone's even in there?" the second killer asked.

The first one thought about it. They all knew what happened at the gym.

"Maybe," he said. "Maybe not. They could have gone into hiding or something. Most likely they know we're coming."

He would have said more, but it was at that point when Que somehow magically appeared at his window and John John at the other window, neither of the killers even had a chance to scream as their bodies were filled with bullets. It was as soon as the shooting quieted down that Joker's doorstep light came on. He opened the door and stepped halfway out.

"Everything alright out there?" he hollered.

"Yeah... Yeah... Everything's good. You can go on back to sleep old man," Que called back.

Joker re-entered his house. Que pulled his phone out as they headed back to the car. He sent a short text and got one back just as quickly.

"Come on.... sun said we can still catch this trip down south," he told John John.

*****

Chalice stood talking with B'Nice as Paris spoke with both Baby Nick and Latoria. They'd already done away with Pocket Change and Rico. And when Paris explained to Chalice the importance of putting Latoria on the team, he couldn't see it any other way. They needed her in case any of them were ever locked up and in the county jail. She was their inside person.

"So bruh... You just hold this shit down." Paris was in the process of explaining. "And if either one of you ever needed something, don't hesitate to ask." He looked at both Baby Nick and Latoria.

"Any questions before I got?" he asked.

"Just one... When do I start getting paid?" Latoria asked.

"Girl... You ain't even did nothing yet," Baby Nick said, but Paris laughed.

He told her as he reached into his pocket and pulled out a roll, "Here you go, Ma." Paris tossed it to her. "You part of the family now and none of our women are hurting for anything. Call my wife, and she'll plug you into her circle."

Latoria looked down at the money she held. "That's what's up, Big Bruh." She smiled.

Paris turned to walk back to where Chalice and B'Nice waited just as the Challenger pulled up behind the three trucks. Que stepped out followed by John John. They all met up where Chalice and B'Nice stood in front of the Range Rover.

"Alright, God. So, how we gon' do this?" Que asked.

Because they all knew that nothing about going after a powerful figurehead in the cartel was going to be easy.

Chalice looked around at his original team, everyone minus Erica that is, and smiled. With these guys, he would go to war with nearly anybody and he felt that his chances of winning were extra high.

"Well... First off, we've got a long ride ahead of us. So, we need to handle that part first. We'll go over the details once we see the layout," he explained, and they all went to get into their rides.

He hadn't told them, but parked three blocks away was their guardian angel keeping a close eye on them. Chalice paused as he looked at the blue Nismo Coupe. He would tell them about Tereasa once they reached Miami. But for now, he didn't worry about it because he already knew they had the green light to take out the Giovani bloodline.

Trai'Quan

Chapter Twenty-Four

It wasn't a house. It wasn't even a mansion. It was a modern-day castle. The large structure was built on almost nineteen acres of land. In a slightly ranch-style design, the estate would have been priced at nine point three million dollars if the owners were trying to sell it. To reach the estate one had to travel a snake-shaped road after they were allowed to pass through the front gates. The road, once it reached the estate, circled into a large arch that curved around a custom-built water fountain that sat in front of the structure. There were no less than thirty armed men who patrolled the estate. All of them are equipped with the best in weaponry. The mansion, which should have been called a castle, had four floors and a mini elevator. There were a total of sixteen bedrooms all on the third and fourth floors. The second floor consisted of a large conference room, a game room, a bar, and an in-house movie theater. While on the first floor all of the basics, kitchen, living, and dining room.

In this house, Felipe lived like he were the king. This was the Giovani Estate. It had been owned by his family since the late 1980s and was rumored to have been the first hone considered for use in the 80's movie *Scarface* with Al Pacino. But for some reason or another, they weren't able to use the house. Nevertheless, Felipe enjoyed it greatly, especially since he had no wife or kids. That gave him plenty of time to throw outrageous parties. Parties that often went on for weeks. And his biggest secret of all was that Felipe preferred the company of men over that of women. He would still be seen out with women, for the sake of his family's image, and even attempted to get one or two of them pregnant. However, that didn't seem to play out well. He would probably have to get a woman artificially inseminated to have a child. Nevertheless, it would only be something to please his father.

Felipe's room was on the fourth floor, which he normally kept empty of guests because he really didn't want anyone stumbling onto his affairs. That, he knew would be bad for public relations. He'd just finished a three men orgy and left the bed with the two men lying upon it. Felipe had to go relieve himself. Too much drink and drugs had him moving around sluggish, but he managed to make it to the bathroom that he was fond of on the fourth floor. The said bathroom had actually been furnished by one of his previous female relatives, who had everything custom imprinted in bright pink. The fabrics were either Chanel, Ferragamo, or Dolce & Gabbana. Felipe felt like the room was designed specifically for him, in secret that is.

Once inside the bathroom, he stepped into the full walk-in shower and turned the water on. He lathered his body and began to shower. While doing this Felipe was having thoughts of what his father had set into motion. By now all of their enemies should be dead and that would force Ms. Swoop to find another ambassador. As he showered, Felipe thought. Who better to lead the cartels than him?

*****

The house was unusually quiet and that was a first. For the past two weeks, it seemed like the party would never end; people would never leave. But now as he rode the glass elevator down, Felipe saw a few people passed out here and there throughout the third floor. There were some scattered in the halls on the second floor.

"Must've been that new ecstasy," he mumbled.

Someone had come to the party last night talking about how good his new version of the drug was. And before you knew it, everyone was trying it. That was one of the reasons he'd indulged in the orgy. That wasn't something he was into. When the elevator reached the first floor, Felipe suddenly became aware that he didn't see any of his servants anywhere. "That's strange," he mumbled. "I thought for sure Mrs. Betty would have something cooking by now." And as he stepped around the corner entering the kitchen, Felipe froze.

"Please..." Tereasa Swoop smiled from where she sat at the counter with a cup of coffee. "Come on in and have a cup."

"What..." Felipe was at a loss for words, yet he moved further into the kitchen and finally saw the body of his servant, Mrs. Betty, lying on the floor in a pool of blood. "Oh my God..."

Tereasa glanced over as she sipped her coffee.

"Yeah, I told the guys not to kill the innocent, but one of them said she tried to hit the alarm."

She hunched her shoulders like 'oh well'.

"How did you get in? There are thirty guards and lord knows how many other people on the second and third floors." Fear was a motivating force driving Felipe's words at that very moment.

"Yeah... You must be a hard sleeper. That or all of that homosexual lovin'..." She smiled. "It took us a while, but everyone except you are dead. I bet you didn't even check your two lovers before you left the bed, did you?"

And she saw in his eyes that she was right. "Don't lose no sleep over it. What's done is done now. But please...have a seat."

Tereasa watched as the gay South American took a seat and looked across the counter in fear.

"I can pretty much guess what you're thinking right now." She smiled.

"You think that because of the old man, you won't die here

this morning."

Felipe watched as she reached to the inside of her windbreaker and removed a Ruger P-90 9 mm semi-automatic, which he saw had a silencer attached to the end of it. Felipe tried his best to swallow the large lump that formed in his throat.

"Yeah, I know right," Tereasa said. "But if it's any consolation to your mind, I won't expose your dirty little secret to the old man. Besides, I don't think his heart would be able to take it."

With that said, Tereasa lifted the gun and aimed directly at Felipe.

"Any last words?" she asked.

"You know my father will find out what happened, and he'll come for you," Felipe told her.

But then Tereasa laughed.

"Honey... Your old man and the rest of his known family is banished from the United States by the rest of the Cartels and by the United States Government. That became effective last night," she stated.

She watched as the light went out of Felipe's eyes. Whatever he thought was going to happen, would never even be whispered.

"Well... It was nice knowing you."

Tereasa pulled the trigger, placing a bullet in the direct center of Felipe's forehead. He was dead before he fell off his seat.

She pulled her phone out and made a call.

"Yeah..." Beck answered.

"I have several bodies at the Giovani Estate. You probably need to send a cleaner," she said.

There was silence.

"What about the fun boy?" Beck asked. They'd long since

knew that Felipe was gay.

"Gone too."

"Alright... Clear your people out. Mine will be there in ten."

"My people are clear, but I'll wait on yours," she said.

"By the way, what about the woman? Is she going to play by our rules or not?" Beck asked.

"She's playing. Let me worry about her. But I need you to put the word out. The Giovani family is no longer allowed in the United States. Revoke all green cards and place a warrant out for the arrest of one Hector Giovani."

"Done. Anything else?" Beck asked.

"Yeah, that Agent Gina Williamson... have her removed from the DEA. Find something domestic for her, but let her keep the same pay."

"Alright...First thing tomorrow," Beck said. "And Swoop?"

"Yeah?"

"How far along is the pregnancy?" he asked.

Tereasa ran her hand across her belly. She was just now starting to show, and Beck already knew who the father was.

"A little over two months," she stated.

"When you hit five months, I'm placing you on leave. Stacy will run things until your back. And Swoop?"

"Yes sir?"

"You did a good job. Your government appreciates every sacrifice you've made. Through you, we'll have an unbreakable hold on your guy and the Cartel Assembly. Good work."

"Thank you, sir."

In the distance, she could hear the cars as they were pulling up to the estate.

"Your cleaners are here. I have to go."

She ended the call. Tereasa thought everything over. Erica knew about the baby, but they hadn't said anything to Chalice yet. That was something she intended to do once all of this was cleaned up. As it now stood, she controlled the entire cartel assembly stateside. She couldn't do anything about what went down in South America. But when their business touched down in her backyard, she had a say-so over what they did with it from that point on.

After all, she was that bitch!

To say that Mustafa was mad, that was an understatement. All of the news he was hearing seemed to be bad news. Both Pocket Change and Rico were gunned down in some type of drive-by shooting. He couldn't prove that Baby Nick had anything to do with it. Especially with him hearing that some more people from the Islands have started showing up. Shit, there were three of them a few cells down from his. They'd just come in a few days ago. Word was, Baby Nick truly did have his spot now. He was moving big work and had even moved in with his baby's mother. Mustafa didn't know what was up with that bitch. Latoria was bumped up to Sargent and no longer worked the floors. He hadn't even seen the bitch and she wasn't returning his calls.

But it's all good though, he thought as he looked at his image in the mirror. He freshened up. He was waiting on the bitch, Drucila, to come through. She was not only bringing him his first package, but he'd just had someone Cash App the bitch two stacks. That's what she said it would cost for him to fuck her. And at the count, she'd told him she would pull up when their shift supervisor went on break.

Mustafa had never paid for pussy before, but being in jail put a nigga under a whole different set of circumstances. *It didn't matter*, he thought. He would get it back out of the bitch when she dropped the pack. He heard the front doors as they slid open and he could hear her keys. She's probably walking around to make it look good. After all, they did have cameras. Mustafa waited patiently, but now that the moment was at hand. It seemed like the bitch was taking her fuckin time and shit.

And then, he heard the keys at his door. Mustafa moved to stand at the back of his cell. But when the key turned, and the lock clicked... Nothing happened at first. Just when he decided to go see what the holdup was, the door was snatched open wide. What he saw wasn't what he'd paid for to see. Standing in the doorway, he saw the three Jamaicans that had come in a few days ago. And all three of them held shanks. Behind them, he saw officer Cortez standing there smiling. It was at that moment he realized her accent was the same as the Jamaicans.

Amazingly, Drucila thought as she stood there and watched her bredren kill Mustafa. The nigga didn't scream. Instead, he took it like a man. Not that screaming would have helped anyway. John John's wife, Alicia, had also gotten a job there and was working the control booth. Sargent Latoria Moss somehow made the power on this floor blink out, so the cameras were down, and it was completely dark on the range. There wouldn't be any eyewitnesses. No, Mustafa had just asked for more than he could handle.

"I guess he didn't know. Island pussy is deadly," Drucila mumbled to herself.

To Be Continued...
Extended Clips 3
Coming

Submission Guideline

Submit the first three chapters of your completed manuscript to ldpsubmissions@gmail.com, subject line: Your book's title. The manuscript must be in a .doc file and sent as an attachment. Document should be in Times New Roman, double spaced and in size 12 font. Also, provide your synopsis and full contact information. If sending multiple submissions, they must each be in a separate email.

Have a story but no way to send it electronically? You can still submit to LDP/Ca$h Presents. Send in the first three chapters, written or typed, of your completed manuscript to:

LDP: Submissions Dept
Po Box 944
Stockbridge, Ga 30281

DO NOT send original manuscript. Must be a duplicate.

Provide your synopsis and a cover letter containing your full contact information.

Thanks for considering LDP and Ca$h Presents.

Coming Soon from Lock Down Publications/Ca$h Presents

BOW DOWN TO MY GANGSTA

By **Ca$h**

TORN BETWEEN TWO

By **Coffee**

THE STREETS STAINED MY SOUL **II**

By **Marcellus Allen**

BLOOD OF A BOSS **VI**

SHADOWS OF THE GAME II

TRAP BASTARD II

By **Askari**

LOYAL TO THE GAME **IV**

By **T.J. & Jelissa**

IF LOVING YOU IS WRONG... **III**

By **Jelissa**

TRUE SAVAGE **VIII**

MIDNIGHT CARTEL IV

DOPE BOY MAGIC IV

CITY OF KINGZ III

By **Chris Green**

BLAST FOR ME **III**

A SAVAGE DOPEBOY III

CUTTHROAT MAFIA III

DUFFLE BAG CARTEL VI

HEARTLESS GOON VI

By **Ghost**

A HUSTLER'S DECEIT III

KILL ZONE **II**

BAE BELONGS TO ME III

A DOPE BOY'S QUEEN III

By **Aryanna**

COKE KINGS V

KING OF THE TRAP II

By **T.J. Edwards**

GORILLAZ IN THE BAY V

3X KRAZY III

De'Kari

THE STREETS ARE CALLING II

Duquie Wilson

KINGPIN KILLAZ IV

STREET KINGS III

PAID IN BLOOD III

CARTEL KILLAZ IV

DOPE GODS III

Hood Rich

SINS OF A HUSTLA II

ASAD

KINGZ OF THE GAME VI

Playa Ray

SLAUGHTER GANG IV

RUTHLESS HEART IV

By Willie Slaughter

THE HEART OF A SAVAGE III

By Jibril Williams

FUK SHYT II

By Blakk Diamond

TRAP QUEEN

By Troublesome

YAYO V

GHOST MOB II

Stilloan Robinson

KINGPIN DREAMS III

By Paper Boi Rari

CREAM II

By Yolanda Moore

SON OF A DOPE FIEND III

By Renta

FOREVER GANGSTA II

GLOCKS ON SATIN SHEETS III

By Adrian Dulan

LOYALTY AIN'T PROMISED III

By Keith Williams

THE PRICE YOU PAY FOR LOVE III

By Destiny Skai

I'M NOTHING WITHOUT HIS LOVE II

SINS OF A THUG II

By Monet Dragun

LIFE OF A SAVAGE IV

MURDA SEASON IV

GANGLAND CARTEL IV

CHI'RAQ GANGSTAS III

By **Romell Tukes**

QUIET MONEY IV

EXTENDED CLIP III

By **Trai'Quan**

THE STREETS MADE ME III

By **Larry D. Wright**

IF YOU CROSS ME ONCE II

ANGEL III

By **Anthony Fields**

FRIEND OR FOE III

By **Mimi**

SAVAGE STORMS III

By **Meesha**

BLOOD ON THE MONEY III

By J-Blunt

THE STREETS WILL NEVER CLOSE II

By K'ajji

NIGHTMARES OF A HUSTLA III

By King Dream

THE WIFEY I USED TO BE II

By Nicole Goosby

IN THE ARM OF HIS BOSS

By Jamila

MONEY, MURDER & MEMORIES II

Malik D. Rice

CONCRETE KILLAZ II

By Kingpen

HARD AND RUTHLESS II

By Von Wiley Hall

LEVELS TO THIS SHYT II

By Ah'Million

MOB TIES II

By SayNoMore

BODYMORE MURDERLAND II

By Delmont Player

Available Now

RESTRAINING ORDER **I & II**

By **CA$H & Coffee**

LOVE KNOWS NO BOUNDARIES **I II & III**

By **Coffee**

RAISED AS A GOON I, II, III & IV

BRED BY THE SLUMS I, II, III

BLAST FOR ME I & II

ROTTEN TO THE CORE I II III

A BRONX TALE I, II, III

DUFFLE BAG CARTEL I II III IV V

HEARTLESS GOON I II III IV V

A SAVAGE DOPEBOY I II

DRUG LORDS I II III

CUTTHROAT MAFIA I II

By **Ghost**

LAY IT DOWN **I & II**

LAST OF A DYING BREED I II

BLOOD STAINS OF A SHOTTA I & II III

By **Jamaica**

LOYAL TO THE GAME I II III

LIFE OF SIN I, II III

By **TJ & Jelissa**

BLOODY COMMAS I & II

SKI MASK CARTEL I II & III

KING OF NEW YORK I II,III IV V

RISE TO POWER I II III

COKE KINGS I II III IV

BORN HEARTLESS I II III IV

KING OF THE TRAP

By **T.J. Edwards**

IF LOVING HIM IS WRONG…I & II

LOVE ME EVEN WHEN IT HURTS I II III

By **Jelissa**

WHEN THE STREETS CLAP BACK I & II III

THE HEART OF A SAVAGE I II

By **Jibril Williams**

A DISTINGUISHED THUG STOLE MY HEART I II & III

LOVE SHOULDN'T HURT I II III IV

RENEGADE BOYS I II III IV

PAID IN KARMA I II III

SAVAGE STORMS I II

By **Meesha**

A GANGSTER'S CODE I &, II III

A GANGSTER'S SYN I II III

THE SAVAGE LIFE I II III

CHAINED TO THE STREETS I II III

BLOOD ON THE MONEY I II

By J-Blunt

PUSH IT TO THE LIMIT

By **Bre' Hayes**

BLOOD OF A BOSS **I, II, III, IV, V**

SHADOWS OF THE GAME

TRAP BASTARD

By **Askari**

THE STREETS BLEED MURDER **I, II & III**

THE HEART OF A GANGSTA I II& III

By **Jerry Jackson**

CUM FOR ME I II III IV V VI

An **LDP Erotica Collaboration**

BRIDE OF A HUSTLA **I II & II**

THE FETTI GIRLS **I, II& III**

CORRUPTED BY A GANGSTA I, II III, IV

BLINDED BY HIS LOVE

THE PRICE YOU PAY FOR LOVE I II

DOPE GIRL MAGIC I II III

By **Destiny Skai**

WHEN A GOOD GIRL GOES BAD

By **Adrienne**

THE COST OF LOYALTY I II III

By Kweli

A GANGSTER'S REVENGE **I II III & IV**

THE BOSS MAN'S DAUGHTERS I II III IV V

A SAVAGE LOVE **I & II**

BAE BELONGS TO ME I II

A HUSTLER'S DECEIT I, II, III

WHAT BAD BITCHES DO I, II, III

SOUL OF A MONSTER I II III

KILL ZONE

A DOPE BOY'S QUEEN I II

By **Aryanna**

A KINGPIN'S AMBITON

A KINGPIN'S AMBITION **II**

I MURDER FOR THE DOUGH

By **Ambitious**

TRUE SAVAGE I II III IV V VI VII

DOPE BOY MAGIC I, II, III

MIDNIGHT CARTEL I II III

CITY OF KINGZ I II

By **Chris Green**

A DOPEBOY'S PRAYER

By **Eddie "Wolf" Lee**

THE KING CARTEL **I, II & III**

By **Frank Gresham**

THESE NIGGAS AIN'T LOYAL **I, II & III**

By **Nikki Tee**

GANGSTA SHYT **I II &III**

By **CATO**

THE ULTIMATE BETRAYAL

By **Phoenix**

BOSS'N UP **I , II & III**

By **Royal Nicole**

I LOVE YOU TO DEATH

By Destiny J

I RIDE FOR MY HITTA

I STILL RIDE FOR MY HITTA

By **Misty Holt**

LOVE & CHASIN' PAPER

By **Qay Crockett**

TO DIE IN VAIN

SINS OF A HUSTLA

By **ASAD**

BROOKLYN HUSTLAZ

By **Boogsy Morina**

BROOKLYN ON LOCK I & II

By **Sonovia**

GANGSTA CITY

By **Teddy Duke**

A DRUG KING AND HIS DIAMOND I & II III

A DOPEMAN'S RICHES

HER MAN, MINE'S TOO I, II

CASH MONEY HO'S

THE WIFEY I USED TO BE

By Nicole Goosby

TRAPHOUSE KING **I II & III**

KINGPIN KILLAZ I II III

STREET KINGS I II

PAID IN BLOOD **I II**

CARTEL KILLAZ I II III

DOPE GODS I II

By **Hood Rich**

LIPSTICK KILLAH **I, II, III**

CRIME OF PASSION I II & III

FRIEND OR FOE I II

By **Mimi**

STEADY MOBBN' **I, II, III**

THE STREETS STAINED MY SOUL

By **Marcellus Allen**

WHO SHOT YA **I, II, III**

SON OF A DOPE FIEND I II

Renta

GORILLAZ IN THE BAY **I II III IV**

TEARS OF A GANGSTA I II

3X KRAZY I II

DE'KARI

TRIGGADALE I II III

Elijah R. Freeman

GOD BLESS THE TRAPPERS I, II, III

THESE SCANDALOUS STREETS I, II, III

Extended Clip 2

FEAR MY GANGSTA I, II, III IV, V

THESE STREETS DON'T LOVE NOBODY I, II

BURY ME A G I, II, III, IV, V

A GANGSTA'S EMPIRE I, II, III, IV

THE DOPEMAN'S BODYGAURD I II

THE REALEST KILLAZ I II III

Tranay Adams

THE STREETS ARE CALLING

Duquie Wilson

MARRIED TO A BOSS... I II III

By Destiny Skai & Chris Green

KINGZ OF THE GAME I II III IV V

Playa Ray

SLAUGHTER GANG I II III

RUTHLESS HEART I II III

By Willie Slaughter

FUK SHYT

By Blakk Diamond

DON'T F#CK WITH MY HEART I II

By Linnea

ADDICTED TO THE DRAMA I II III

IN THE ARM OF HIS BOSS II

By Jamila

YAYO I II III IV

A SHOOTER'S AMBITION I II

By S. Allen

TRAP GOD I II III

By Troublesome
FOREVER GANGSTA
GLOCKS ON SATIN SHEETS I II
By Adrian Dulan
TOE TAGZ I II III
LEVELS TO THIS SHYT
By Ah'Million
KINGPIN DREAMS I II
By Paper Boi Rari
CONFESSIONS OF A GANGSTA I II III
By Nicholas Lock
I'M NOTHING WITHOUT HIS LOVE
SINS OF A THUG
By Monet Dragun
CAUGHT UP IN THE LIFE I II III
By Robert Baptiste
NEW TO MONEY, MURDER & MEMORIES
THE GAME I II III
By **Malik D. Rice**
LIFE OF A SAVAGE I II III
A GANGSTA'S QUR'AN I II III
MURDA SEASON I II III
GANGLAND CARTEL I II III
CHI'RAQ GANGSTAS I II
By **Romell Tukes**
LOYALTY AIN'T PROMISED I II
By Keith Williams

QUIET MONEY I II III

THUG LIFE I II

EXTENDED CLIP I II

By **Trai'Quan**

THE STREETS MADE ME I II

By **Larry D. Wright**

THE ULTIMATE SACRIFICE I, II, III, IV, V, VI

KHADIFI

IF YOU CROSS ME ONCE

ANGEL I II

By **Anthony Fields**

THE LIFE OF A HOOD STAR

By **Ca$h & Rashia Wilson**

THE STREETS WILL NEVER CLOSE

By **K'ajji**

CREAM

By **Yolanda Moore**

NIGHTMARES OF A HUSTLA I II

By **King Dream**

CONCRETE KILLAZ

By **Kingpen**

HARD AND RUTHLESS

By **Von Wiley Hall**

GHOST MOB II

Stilloan Robinson

MOB TIES

By **SayNoMore**

BODYMORE MURDERLAND

By Delmont Player

BOOKS BY LDP'S CEO, CA$H

TRUST IN NO MAN

TRUST IN NO MAN 2

TRUST IN NO MAN 3

BONDED BY BLOOD

SHORTY GOT A THUG

THUGS CRY

THUGS CRY 2

THUGS CRY 3

TRUST NO BITCH

TRUST NO BITCH 2

TRUST NO BITCH 3

TIL MY CASKET DROPS

RESTRAINING ORDER

RESTRAINING ORDER 2

IN LOVE WITH A CONVICT

LIFE OF A HOOD STAR

Trai'Quan